Four years ago, a night of forbidden passion between Remi and Julien, the heirs of two powerful and competitive horse racing families, led to a feud that is threatening to ruin both farms. Now Remi must find Julien again —but when she does, her need for Julien is just as strong and just as forbidden...

THE ORIGINAL SINNERS PULP LIBRARY

Vintage paperback-inspired editions of standalone novels and novellas from *USA Today* bestseller Tiffany Reisz's million-copy selling Original Sinners erotic romance series. Learn more: tiffanyreisz.com.

THE ORIGINAL SINNERS
PULP LIBRARY

SEIZE
THE NIGHT

SEIZE THE NIGHT

TIFFANY REISZ

8TH CIRCLE PRESS • LOUISVILLE, KY

Previously published by Harlequin Books/Mills & Boon
as part of the *Captivated* duology

Cover design by Andrew Shaffer

Front cover image contains photos used under license
from Shutterstock

Mass-Market Paperback ISBN: 978-1-949769-49-4

Also available as an eBook and Audiobook

Second Edition

The boy in blue started the fight but the boy in red looked determined to finish it. Swearing turned to yelling turned to shoving. Remi fished her phone out of her messenger bag. She called the security office and two minutes later the fight was over and both young men—college kids by the looks of them —were being escorted away. Too much alcohol and testosterone. Too little good sense.

Remi felt the needle-prick of her conscience. She couldn't judge them, tempting as it was. She'd been in college not that long ago, and remembered being that stupid. Remembered it all too well.

Still, it made no sense to her. Two guys in opposing jerseys fighting at a football game made sense. Or even a baseball or a basketball game. But this was Verona Downs. Who got into fights over racehorses? Bizarre. Bizarre was the only word for it.

Bizarre was also the only word for the man entering the grandstand and making his way toward her. He was wearing all black, as usual, right down to his underwear (assuming he had any on today). His shirt was untucked, because that was the only way he ever wore button-downs. Under the black sunglasses lurked intelligent blue eyes usually narrowed in suspicion or derision. Most of the women in the stands followed his progress. She didn't blame them. He was mid-thirties, annoyingly handsome, and wasn't smiling. He had an *I can't wait to rock your world in bed and then make you regret you ever met me* look about him. Women fell for that look often. She hadn't. She had zero desire to sleep with him. He was Merrick Dearborn, her assistant. And of course she didn't want to sleep with him. She'd met him.

"Why, pray tell, am I sitting among the plebeians?" Merrick asked as he took his seat next to her. They must have made an odd pair. He looked like a rock star, while her attire—

faded jeans, tailored plaid shirt, cowboy boots —was more rodeo star.

"This is not ancient Rome, and these are not plebeians. These are people just like us," Remi said as she made a notation in her leather journal. "And you're sitting here because your boss wants your sunshiny self sitting right next to her."

"We have that nice Arden Farms private box right over there," Merrick said, pointing at the clubhouse balcony section where all the horse owners had private air-conditioned boxes. "This 'man of the people' routine of yours is infringing on my creature comforts."

"This is not a 'man of the people' routine," Remi said. "First of all, I *am* the people, not *of* the people. You and I are people, whether you want to admit it or not. Second, I am not a man."

"Prove it," Merrick said with a sly smile.

"I'm not sleeping with you. I'm your employer. You are my assistant."

"According to string theory, an infinite multiverse exists—and in at least one of them, we're sleeping together."

"You just used quantum physics to hit on me. I'm almost impressed."

"Impressed enough to sleep with me?" Merrick asked.

"No."

Merrick shrugged. He seemed merely philosophical about her refusal and not the least disappointed. For all his quantum flirting, Merrick's interest in her was merely mechanical. And she had no interest in him at all. She was twenty-six and he thirty-six. To her he was like an older brother. An older brother she paid to do whatever she told him to do. The best sort of older brother. The type she could fire.

Remi's cell phone buzzed in her bag. She fished it out and looked at the name. Now she remembered why she'd hired Merrick.

"Brian Roseland." Remi handed the phone to Merrick.

"You want me to do the thing?" he asked.

"Please and thank you."

"Yell-o?" Merrick said, taking the call for her. "No, Remi's not here right now. She's on a date."

Remi covered her mouth to stifle a laugh. Her? On a date on a Thursday afternoon at four? Good thing Merrick was a better liar than she was.

"She's been gone all week, Mr. Roseland," Merrick said. "It's that kind of date. One with traveling and exotic locations and them sticking body parts into each other."

Remi grabbed for the phone. Merrick jerked it out of her way.

"But I'll tell her you called once she gets back from her weeklong exotic locale sex date." Merrick tugged her ponytail to annoy her. It worked.

Merrick ended the call and handed her the phone. "I told Roseland you were on an exotic locale weeklong sex date," he said.

"Yes, I heard that part as I was sitting next to you the entire time. Did you have to go into that much detail?" she demanded.

"Look, Boss," Merrick said, "either learn how to lie to people or leave me alone when you make me do your lying for you."

"Fine. Thank you for getting rid of him. Third time he's called me this week," she said.

"Didn't you break up with him?"

"Yeah, but he still calls all the time. Maybe if he thinks I'm on a weeklong exotic locale sex date he'll finally get the hint that it's completely over."

Remi dropped her phone back in her bag

just as the post parade began. The outriders trotted alongside the jockeys astride their race-horses. She saw her own Arden Farms' jockey, Mike Alvarez, in his red and white silks, throw a smile at the crowd as he and their three-year-old filly Shenanigans passed the grandstand.

"Boss, are you ever going to tell me why you dumped Roseland?" Merrick asked, as she made a note in her journal.

"My private life is on a need-to-know basis and you do not need to know."

"Please? I'll whimper. Don't make me whimper." He whimpered.

"Do you really care?" she asked. "Or is this just perverse curiosity about my sex life?"

"I care desperately in a perversely curious way about your sex life," Merrick said. "You never tell me anything about your personal life. You don't hit on me. You ignore me when I hit on you. You keep our work relationship professional no matter how hard I try to make it unprofessional. It's like you have integrity or something and quite frankly, I'm sick of it."

Remi closed her journal. "If I tell you will you shut up for two whole minutes during the race?"

"Two minutes? I can do that. Talk," Merrick ordered.

"When I started dating Brian, I thought he was a really nice guy," she began.

"No wonder you dumped him," Merrick said. She glowered at him. He whimpered in response.

"I happen to like nice guys," she said, and a face from her past flashed in front of her eyes. A young, handsome, smiling face—near-black eyes, dark red hair, a smile both sweet and striking. She kicked the memory out of her mind—a futile gesture. She knew it would only gallop back into her brain. "In fact, I love nice guys. It just turned out Brian wasn't a nice guy."

Merrick pushed his sunglasses up on top of his head and stared at her. "If he hurt you, you tell me right now, Remi. If he got rough with you I will get rough with him. That prick can watch the horses race from his boxed seats in Hell."

He only called her Remi in his rare deadly serious moods. He'd probably called her by her first name all of twice in two years. The rest of the time she was just "Boss."

She shook her head. "No, he didn't hurt me," she said, touched by Merrick's devotion to her. They harassed and insulted each other, but at the heart of their working relationship was a solid core of respect and loyalty. And amused exasperation on her part. "I promise. I'd kick his ass if he tried. It was just that... So, three months ago, Brian and I were...you know..."

"Twerking?"

"Fucking. And the condom broke. I'm on birth control, but I still panicked. Abject white-knuckle panic."

"Even the thought of having a baby with Brian terrified me. I couldn't imagine spending Christmas with him, much less marrying him and having kids. It was a horrible thought. So we broke up."

She spoke matter-of-factly but the break-up had been anything but matter-of-fact. Brian had been furious, accusatory, demanding to know if she was cheating on him. He'd been so bitterly angry he'd scared her, and from that moment on, she refused to see him or speak to him. Breaking up with him and his ensuing profanity-laden tantrum had shown her why her instincts to dump him had been so dead-on.

"That's the whole story?" Merrick asked, sounding skeptical.

"That's it. I broke up with him. He threw a hissy fit about it."

"Well, you are *easily* the second or third most beautiful woman in north-central Kentucky."

"Thank you for that regionally-specific compliment," she said. "Now shut up. It's post time."

Merrick went silent as all six horses were slotted into the starting gate. Any second now the bell would ring and the horses would burst from the gates. It was just an ordinary race on a Thursday afternoon at Verona Downs. Not even a stakes race. But it as so packed it could have been the Derby. At least fifty people had brought homemade signs reading I CALL SHENANIGANS! Did these people not realize that horses, unlike football or baseball players, could not read?

Remi held her breath.

The bell rang and the horses exploded onto the track in a furor of pounding hooves and streaming colors. The crowd cheered and clapped and roared. She and Merrick watched the race in silence.

After two minutes and a mile and a half, Shenanigans of Arden Farms was declared the unofficial winner. She should have been happy that their champion filly had won the race. A nice purse, a sweet victory, another trophy in the trophy room...

"You don't look happy, precious," Merrick said and put two fingers on either side of her face, forcing her lips into a smile. She gave him the most glaring of death glares. "Your little pony won her race. Smile like you mean it."

The outrider led Mike and Shenanigans on a victory lap.

"Let's go," she said.

"Thank God," Merrick said as they stood up. "I'm starting to sweat. It's October. I don't let myself sweat in October."

She grabbed her things, and Merrick let her out into the aisle. He followed behind her as she strode to the rails.

"Have you noticed anything weird?" she asked him.

"Yes. Definitely. What the hell does that woman have on top of her head? A sailboat?" He pointed at a lady walking past their section. "Ahoy there!" he shouted at the woman in the white hat with the voluminous veil. "No one can see over your damn schooner! Full steam ahead!"

The woman hadn't heard—or was ignoring him—but Remi scolded her assistant anyway. "Merrick, please behave yourself."

"Why? These are the cheap seats. Nobody knows that YOU'RE REMI MONTGOMERY AND YOUR FAMILY OWNS SHENANIGANS, THE WINNING HORSE." Merrick said that last sentence so loudly everyone in a twenty-yard radius heard him.

"And you wonder why I won't ever sleep with you," she whispered to him.

"AND YOU AND I AREN'T SLEEPING TOGETHER," Merrick said, still in his unnecessarily booming voice. Everyone in the grandstands stared at them as they walked down to the viewing area in front of the track.

Remi slid her bag over her shoulder as they headed to the clubhouse. "Remind me why I hired you again."

"Because I don't give a fuck about horse racing. Also I'm brilliant and you find me the sexiest man alive."

"Two out of three ain't bad. Come here, I want to show you something," she said, pausing at the track to watch the jockey weigh-in. The results of the race wouldn't be official until the jockeys were weighed.

"It's about time. But let's find a stall so we can have some privacy for our first time. I want it to be as awkward and uncomfortable as possible for the both of us."

She opened her bag and handed him a magazine.

"Wow," Merrick said, a word she'd never heard pass his lips before. Merrick was not easily impressed. "You don't see horses on the cover of *Sports Illustrated* very often. Then again, I only subscribe for the swimsuit issue."

Remi stood next to him as they stared at the cover—Shenanigans, her family's chestnut filly, and Hijinks, the Capital Hills colt, barreling down the center of the Verona Downs track straight at the camera. The picture had been snapped in the final stretch of the Lexington Stakes, a glorious action shot of two beautiful beasts running their guts out.

"Look at that headline. *The New Civil War—Hijinks V Shenanigans in the horse racing rivalry of the century*," Remi read aloud, trying not to roll her eyes at the hyperbole.

Merrick handed her the magazine. "That'll sell some t-shirts."

"This article is ridiculous," Remi said, flipping through the pages. "It's all about the vicious rivalry between Arden Farms and Capital Hills—two of the oldest Kentucky horse farms. Everyone's picking a side—Team Shenanigans versus Team Hijinks."

"I'm still Team Edward."

"I saw a fight today right by the rails. It was between two guys, one wearing an Arden shirt, the other guy in a Capital Hills shirt. After this feature, the entire racing world will be betting on Shenanigans and Hijinks now. They're even selling Hijinks and Shenanigans Beanie Babies."

"Now that's just sick."

"Tell me about it. These horses are turning into money trees."

"You say that like it's a bad thing. Shenanigans is your family's horse," he reminded her. "More notoriety, better attendance, better press, more money...more money for me, your faithful assistant who deserves a raise. Should I write this down for you?"

"Write this down for me," she said, handing Merrick a pen and her journal. "One-hundred million and two-hundred million. Got it?"

He held up the page where he'd written the figures. "So?"

"One-hundred million is how much money is bet on the Kentucky Derby. Two-hundred million is how much is bet on the Breeders Cup."

"And I wrote them down why?"

Remi shook her head and turned to the Winner's Circle. Her mother and father stood next to Shenanigans while the assembled press frantically took pictures.

"You wrote them down because I want you to see how much money there is in horse racing."

"Fine. I'll buy a goddamn pony."

"You shouldn't buy a goldfish, Merrick. That's not my point."

"What's your point then?"

She exhaled hard and shook her head. She'd been dreading this question because she'd been dreading the answer to it. Still, Merrick was the one person in her life she trusted right now, so she might as well tell him.

"My parents bought a new farm a couple months ago," she said. "Satellite farm. Five-hundred acres."

"So?"

"They paid cash. Ten million dollars. We shouldn't have ten million dollars in cash lying around."

"And?"

"I don't know," she admitted. "But we shouldn't have that much money lying around. Capital Hills seems to have had a windfall too. The auctions were this week—they dropped ten million the first three days."

"Damn."

"That's kind of a coincidence, isn't it? They suddenly have ten million dollars? We suddenly have ten million dollars?"

"A slightly suspicious coincidence," Merrick said, narrowing his eyes at her parents.

"That's what I was thinking."

"Rivalries always make for money and headlines. But Merrick, I don't know. Something doesn't smell right about this. And trust me, my family and the Capital Hills family aren't in anything together. They hate each other."

"I've noticed that."

"But still, I think someone at Arden and someone at Capital Hill might be stoking this rivalry in the press for a reason."

"What reason?" Merrick asked. "Money?"

"Is there any other reason?" Remi asked, feeling sick to her stomach even saying that much. "Tyson Balt was at our house last night."

"He owns Verona Downs, right? 'V.D.' for

short? He really should have rethought that name. What about him?"

"Balt's been promoting the hell out of the Verona Stakes race. Shenanigans and Hijinks are the two favorites already."

"You think your family is getting the money from Balt?"

"Something's not right," was all she would say.

Merrick pursed his lips and whistled.

"I don't have the evidence yet. It's only a hunch," Remi said.

"You really want to dig this hole? You might end up falling into it, Boss."

"I know," she said, her stomach tightening. "But if my hunch is right, there's a fraud being perpetuated here at Verona. I can't look the other way even if my own family is involved."

"We should talk to someone at Capital Hills. What's their name? The Brites?" Merrick asked.

Remi swallowed. Heat rushed to her face. "Yes," she said, her voice neutral. "The Capital farm has been in the Brite family for 150 years."

"The parents are out since they're probably in on this, whatever it is," Merrick said. "And we can't talk to the daughters. I banged two out of three of them and didn't call after."

"Wait. When did that happen?"

"What was that thing with the big hats you dragged me to in May?"

"The Kentucky Derby?"

"That."

"You had a threesome with two of the Brite daughters at the Kentucky Derby?"

"You say that like it's a bad thing."

"This is why I can't take you anywhere. Okay, so the sisters are out."

"Two out of three are. Anyone else?" Merrick asked. "A trainer maybe? Maybe we can find a stable boy you can bat your tits and flash your eyelashes at."

"I doubt a groom would know anything."

"A higher up then? A secretary?"

Remi shifted uncomfortably as her parents smiled for the dozens of cameras in the winner's circle. Even Shenanigans seemed to be smiling.

"Well...I guess we can talk to Julien Brite," Remi said. A tiny tremor passed through her body as his name passed her lips.

"Which one's Julien?"

"Julien is the son. The youngest in the family."

"Never heard of him," Merrick said.

"He's not in the business," Remi said. "Not sure why. I don't even know where he lives now."

"You know him?"

"Sort of."

Merrick narrowed his eyes at her. "Can you trust him?"

"He's the only member of the Brite family who doesn't hate me," Remi said, hoping that was true.

"He sounds like our guy then. You want to find him and go talk to him about this stupid rivalry?"

"Oh, he already knows about the rivalry," Remi said with a heavy sigh. "But yes, he's probably the only one in the Brite family we can talk to."

Remi stepped away from the rails and headed toward the clubhouse.

"You said Julien isn't involved in the business. How do you know he knows all about the rivalry?" Merrick asked as the crowd ahead parted for them. The grandstand might not know who she and Merrick were, but the clubhouse crowd certainly did. Tyson Balt, the owner of Verona Downs, eyed her warily. The feeling was entirely mutual. And up in the boxes she saw Mr. and Mrs. Brite giving an interview to a reporter as a camera recorded their every word. She glanced up at them. They glared down at her with unmistakable abject loathing.

"Because," Remi sighed. "Four years ago, Julien and I accidentally started it."

On Friday morning, Remi and Merrick boarded an airplane to take them to Julien Brite. Halfway through the flight Remi realized she'd been digging her hand into Merrick's knee for the past two hours. Flying didn't scare her. She'd spent too many years on the back of high-jumping horses to be afraid of a little altitude. But even after four hours of smooth sailing, Remi remained a rapidly fraying knot of tension.

"Boss? You okay?" Merrick asked as he signaled the flight attendant for another drink. He was having way too much fun in First Class, much more fun than she was. "I mean, I don't mind that you're squeezing my knee so hard I can't feel my calf, but there are other body parts I could direct your attention to, if you're interested."

"Steady as she goes." Remi snatched the vodka from her assistant and chugged it.

"Whoa, Nellie." Merrick took it back. "We've got five hours left on this flight."

"Sorry," she said. "Take it. I'm fine."

"Yeah, you seem real fucking fine. What's wrong?"

"Nothing."

"How many times do I have to tell you that you're the world's worst liar?" Merrick asked. "You're stressed about seeing this Julien guy again."

"A smidge," she said. "A skoosh."

"Are you going to tell me why?"

She shook her head. "Not if you won't let me have your vodka."

He gave her the vodka. "Sip it and talk. You can't say something like 'Julien and I started this rivalry' and sashay off all dramatic-like without telling me the story."

"It's a humiliating story," Remi said.

"Miss?" Merrick addressed the passing flight attendant. "I'm going to need some popcorn."

"Merrick."

"Talk," he said. "And don't leave out any juicy details."

"I'm leaving out all the juicy details," she said. "You get the bare bones."

"Is there boning involved in the bare bones?"

"Almost," she said, wincing. She took a steadying breath and focused her attention on the hum of the airplane engines. It comforted her, the sound of the engines reminding her she was thousands of miles and years away from the time and place of her greatest humiliation.

"Go on..." Merrick said.

"This was back when I was in college. I'd come home for Christmas, and Mom and Dad dragged me to a big Christmas party at The Rails."

"That's that huge horse farm in Versailles, yes?"

"Yes, bigger than Capital Hills and Arden put together."

"Got it. So it's Christmas. It's a party. You're what? Twenty?"

"Twenty-two," she said. "It was a formal party so I had an excuse to buy an awesome dress. Jade strappy thing."

"Did it make your tits look good?"

"Spectacular," she said.

"Continue, please."

"Anyway," she said and paused to sip Merrick's vodka. She hated the stuff but needed a little liquid fortification. "I was there about an hour before I saw this gorgeous guy. He was standing on the other side of the room talking to a big hotshot Kentucky basketball player. So I assumed he was a Kentucky student, probably a freshman. He looked about eighteen, and he was drinking a glass of white wine. And he looked handsome in his tuxedo. He had messy red hair. I couldn't take my eyes off him."

"Gross. Don't touch people with your eyeballs."

"*Figuratively* couldn't take my eyes off him," Remi continued. "He was so beautiful that I had to chug a whole glass of wine just to work up the courage to go talk to him."

"And you did, and he was smart and funny and nice and all that boring shit women love?"

"All that and more," Remi said. "We walked through the house together. Gorgeous house. Every room decorated in a different Christmas theme. It was like something out of a fairy tale or a movie. I'd never seen anything like it, never felt anything like it. The night was perfect. Ever have a moment so perfect that you know you'll remember it the rest of your life while you're still living in the moment?"

Remi closed her eyes and found herself once more back in that house on that night. She and Julien stood by the fireplace mantel that was lined with a dozen yellow candles in antique brass candleholders. The room was filled with antique toys and a tree that soared all the way to the cathedral ceiling. The silver and gold stars on the tree reflected the dancing light from the fireplace. The moment was everything she'd ever wanted for Christmas but hadn't known to ask for.

"This guy must have been special," Merrick said.

"He was." Remi knew she was the world's worst liar. Might as well tell the truth. "I didn't know how special he was because he only told me his first name—Julien. We talked about everything and nothing. I don't even remember what we talked about. I just remember him telling me he thought I looked beautiful. Before I knew it, there we were, standing under the mistletoe."

"Best kiss ever?" Merrick asked.

"Best kiss ever," she agreed, remembering how Julien's lips had shivered lightly at the first gentle contact. The gentleness quickly turned to passion and before she knew it, her arms were around his back and his mouth was on her neck, at her ear, at her throat. Every Christmas since then she'd thought of Julien. The lights, the tree, the scent of pine and candles... Maybe that's why she couldn't imagine spending Christmas with Brian Roseland. Christmas was already claimed by Julien.

"I'm guessing the inevitable happened," Merrick said.

"We found an empty guest room. I thought I remembered locking the door behind us."

Merrick cringed. "I see where this is going..."

Remi nodded, her face flushing hot at the memory. "We kissed for a long time. Julien seemed a little nervous, and I didn't want to rush things. But then he unzipped the back of my dress and I unbuttoned his shirt...and his pants...and then."

"And then?"

"And then while I was touching him, he said something weird and I stopped."

"Weird? Did he deny the Holocaust or something?"

"He said, 'This feels better than I ever dreamed it would.'"

Merrick cocked his head to the side. "Ever *dreamed* it would? You mean he'd never had a girl's hand on his cock before?"

"Exactly," she said. "So I immediately sobered up and asked him if he was a virgin."

"Oh fuck," Merrick said.

"Merrick, I was half-naked on a bed with the virginal son of one of the most powerful families in Thoroughbred racing. Legal? Yeah. Barely."

"Oops."

"Two seconds after I told him we had to stop, the door opened. My dress was down, his jacket was off, his shirt was open, his pants were unzipped...and his mother saw it all."

Merrick's eyes went comically wide. Remi would have laughed but for the pain the memory still caused her.

"How bad was it?" he asked.

She appreciated that he seemed to understand the gravity of the situation instead of making Mrs. Robinson jokes.

"Bad. Julien's mom had had a little too much Christmas punch. It turned into a screaming match that everyone at the party heard."

"Oh, that's bad."

"Very bad. My parents showed up and started defending me. His parents called me every ugly name in the book. My father told Julien's father, 'Sir, control your wife.' And five minutes later, they were fighting. Like, physically fighting. Dad gave Mr. Brite a black eye and Mr. Brite gave Dad a bloody nose. It's a miracle no one called the cops."

"Damn."

"The moms pulled the dads off each other but that almost turned into a cat fight until Mr. and Mrs. Railey showed up and calmed everyone down. Poor Julien was begging everyone to just shut up and leave us alone so he and I could talk. Instead, his parents dragged him from the room, and he's apologizing to me the entire time. 'I'm so sorry, Remi. I'm so sorry...'"

She could still hear his hurt, humiliated words ringing in her ears.

"And that started the feud?" Merrick asked.

"That was the beginning. My parents were furious at the Brites for making a scene at the party and accusing me of seducing their baby boy. The Brites were furious at my parents because my parents blamed Julien for pretending he was my age. He didn't lie, for the record. I didn't ask him. Never occurred to me until it was almost too late. And I just stood there in shock, saying nothing and feeling like I was going to puke and trying to get my dad not to kill his dad. I didn't get to talk to him, tell him I was sorry, tell him goodbye even. It was awful."

"You didn't do anything illegal," Merrick said. "Right?"

She nodded. "But still, he was their baby and I was Jezebel."

"So you never saw Julien again, I'm assuming."

"My parents forbade me from contacting him. I haven't seen him since that night. Not even at any of the races." And she'd looked. At every race she'd looked. When their families had ripped them apart that night, it had left an open wound in her heart.

"Where did he go?"

She shrugged and tried not to care that she hadn't seen or heard from him in four years. "He disappeared. And that was that. Except his family still hasn't forgiven me for almost seducing their son, and my family still hasn't forgiven them for publicly humiliating me at the party."

"Have you forgiven him?" Merrick asked.

Remi smiled. "Julien didn't do anything wrong. And while his mom was going batshit crazy on me, calling me every possible variation of slut, whore, and harlot, he stood up to her and his dad and defended me. He'd be twenty-one now. I keep thinking I should...but it doesn't matter. It was a long time ago."

Merrick looked at her with searching serious eyes. "You miss him," he said.

Remi didn't bother to deny it. "I had a perfect moment with him. You don't get many of those in your life."

"This was four years ago? You'd think your families would be over it by now."

"Judging by all the smack talk in the news, they aren't. In that *SI* interview, Mrs. Brite called us the 'white trash' farm."

"Classy."

"Dad called the Brites 'stuck-up snobs.' I'm really hoping Julien hasn't read that article."

"So what are you going to do when you see Julien again? Jump him?"

Remi laughed at the ludicrousness of the suggestion. She was en route to Paris to tell

Julien their parents might be conspiring to fix races. Hardly cause for an erotic reunion.

"I'll do what I should have done years ago," she said. "I'll tell him I'm sorry."

―――

After what felt like a year in the air, the plane landed. They checked into their hotel and Remi gave Merrick the night off. It was Saturday after all. And all she wanted to do was sleep and recover from the flight. Merrick, however, had other plans.

"*Vive la France*, remember?" Merrick grabbed her by the upper arms and forced a kiss on each of her cheeks. "When in Paris, do as the Parisians do."

"What do the Parisians do?"

"I don't know," he admitted. "But I'm hoping it involves getting Parisian drunk and getting Parisian laid. Not necessarily in that Parisian order."

"I'm not drinking with you. Or any of the other options."

"We need to find this Brite boy of yours. My sources tell me he's a short Parisian cab ride away."

"Are you going to put 'Parisian' in front of

every noun until we leave?" Remi asked as Merrick hailed a taxi.

"That would be a Parisian *yes*. I mean, '*oui*.'"

Not only was Merrick refusing to take the night off, but he wanted to get the "business" part of their business trip over with right away. Somehow, Remi—sleep-deprived, annoyed, and anxious—managed not to murder him during the ten minutes between their hotel and Julien's building.

"I think this is it." Merrick said when the cab stopped in front of a nondescript three-story building. He paid the driver, which Remi thought was an unusually gallant gesture until she noticed Merrick was using her credit card. They stepped out onto a side street off the Rue de Furstemberg.

Merrick half-escorted, half-dragged her to the door. "I think this is it. My sources tell me this is it," he said. "And by 'sources' I mean the Brite family housekeeper."

"Are you sure?" she asked. "I can't imagine any of the Brite family staying in someplace so normal. Well, normal for Paris, I mean."

"This has to be it. I paid ten whole dollars for his address."

"Your sources are cheap dates," Remi said. "Let's hope we got your money's worth."

She rang the buzzer and dusted off her high school French.

"*Bonjour?*" came a woman's voice through the speaker. Woman? At Julien's house on a Saturday night?

"*Bonjour,*" Remi said, trying not to be bothered by the elegant voice. "Julien Brite, *s'il vous plait?*"

"Your accent is terrible," the woman answered in English.

Remi laughed. "It's French by way of a Kentucky high school. Is Julien in?"

"He might be," the woman said in a clipped tone. She had something of an accent too but neither French nor Kentuckian. "Who are you?"

"My name is Remi Montgomery of Arden Farms. And—"

"Come up please," the woman said before Remi could even finish her speech.

She looked at Merrick who smiled at her in return.

"Look at you, Boss," he said. "You're famous."

The door buzzed and they headed up the stairs to an apartment on the third floor. Remi knocked and a woman answered the door. She looked about mid-thirties and was clearly of Indian descent even though her clothes—a boat neck shirt, white scarf, and stylish slacks —were pure Parisian chic. And she was beautiful beyond words. So beautiful even Merrick had gone speechless—something of a miracle.

"Oh, holy Parisian shit," Merrick finally said. So much for speechless.

"Excuse me?" the woman asked.

"You'll have to forgive Merrick here," Remi said, slapping Merrick on the back— hard. "You're beautiful, and he's a horrible person. Bad combination."

"Forgiven," she said. "Salena Kar. I work for Julien. You're Remi Montgomery?"

"She is," Merrick said. "And I'm Merrick Dearborn. I work for Remi. It's like destiny, isn't it?"

"What is?" Salena asked as she waved them into the apartment. Remi noticed Salena was barefoot so she slipped off her own shoes and set them by the door.

"I work for her. You work for Julien. It's like we belong together, right?" Merrick said.

"Are you in love with me?" Salena asked, seemingly nonplussed by Merrick's enthusiasm.

"Not yet, but give me five or six minutes and I'll get there."

Salena nodded gracefully. "Take your time," she said, leading them into a living room. While the apartment building had appeared cramped and unremarkable on the outside, inside Remi discovered Julien's home, while not grand, was the perfect mix of classic and cozy.

"How can we help you, Miss Montgomery?" Salena asked.

"Please, call me Remi. I'm sorry for the intrusion. I need to talk to Julien for a few minutes, and then we'll be gone."

"I'll get him for you," she said. "He's in his office."

The woman started to leave the room but paused and turned back around. "He's mentioned you before," she said. "Lovely to put a face to the reputation."

"Bad reputation," Remi said, trying not to blush or wince.

"Quite the opposite," Salena said. She gave Remi a wink and left the room.

"What do you think she does for Julien?" Merrick whispered after Salena had disappeared.

"I don't know. She might be his assistant

so she probably does for him what you do for me."

"Annoy the piss out of you constantly and make you wish you'd never set eyes on me?" Merrick said.

"Among other useful tasks."

"She's the most beautiful woman I've ever seen in my life," Merrick said, sounding surprisingly sincere. "Can I have her?"

"She's a human being. I can't buy her for you."

"If you loved me you would help me," he said, staring at the door Salena had just passed through.

"I don't love you."

She started to pat him on the knee but paused mid-pat when Julien Brite stepped into the doorway of the living room.

"I have to say," Julien began, a crooked smile on his face, "I'm really glad my parents aren't here right now."

He looked at her, and Remi felt something catch in her chest at the sight of him leaning in his doorway, arms crossed and with amusement glimmering in his dark eyes.

"We made sure they weren't going to be visiting you before we booked the trip," Remi said. "And hello. Nice to see you again."

"Really nice to see you again," Julien said, still smiling. He wore jeans and a plain red t-shirt, no shoes, no socks.

"How have you been, Julien?" Remi asked, torn between the desire to stay safely next to Merrick or to walk to Julien and get an even better look at him. He hadn't lost all his teenage lankiness although his shoulders were certainly broader. His hair had darkened to a deeper shade of red and was longer now and artfully mussed. He looked older, definitely. But more than that, he looked chiseled, as if he had walked ten thousand miles across a desert and the wind and sand had worn his adolescent innocence away.

"I'm not dead," he said and laughed as if he'd made a joke. "So I'm good. You?"

"Great. Good. Also not dead."

"You're a little far from home, aren't you?" Julien asked.

"I could say the same to you," Remi said as she finally stood up and walked over to him. "Merrick said you'd moved to Paris and I thought—"

"Paris, Kentucky," he said. "How do you think I tricked my family into letting me move here?"

"Smart," she said.

He smiled again and held out his hand to her. Remi took it and a slight tremor passed through her body when her hand met his. The last time she'd touched him had been far more intimate than a handshake.

"I'm really sorry to show up on your doorstep," she said, Julien's hand still in hers. She was strangely reluctant to let it go.

"I'm not sorry at all. Mom said you're Arden's manager now?"

"Your mother told you about my promotion?"

"Oh yeah," Julien said as Salena appeared in the doorway behind him. She put her hand on his hip to indicate she needed to pass by him, and he shifted the necessary six inches. The subtle gesture spoke of an intimacy between them. Maybe Salena and Julien were more than mere employer/employee.

Remi didn't like that thought.

"Mom keeps me up on all the Bluegrass gossip whether I want to know it or not," Julien said. "I know about your promotion. I know that your parents bought a satellite farm outside Versailles. I know the man sitting on my couch staring at Salena is the infamous Merrick Dearborn."

Merrick lowered his sunglasses and looked Julien in the eye. "It's my pleasure."

Julien snorted. "According to my mother, you're a Harvard computer genius who knows nothing about horses. She says you creep everyone out in Kentucky because you wear black sunglasses all the time. Although two of my three sisters seem to like you for some reason..."

"Your sisters are saints," Merrick said quickly. "At least I assume so. I don't believe I've met them. In fact, I didn't even know you had sisters. They must have been speaking of another Merrick Dearborn."

Remi sighed. "I apologize for my assistant," she said to Julien. "We'll be out of your hair soon. I wanted to talk to you for about ten minutes, and then we'll leave you alone."

"You really don't have to leave me alone," Julien said. "But if you get topless again, please make sure the door's locked this time."

Remi laughed, and she knew she was blushing like a teenager in love. Luckily, Julien was polite enough not to mention the blush.

Unluckily, Merrick wasn't. "Stop blushing, Boss. You're the December in the

May/December, remember?" He paused. "Wait. That rhymed."

"Merrick, you're fired," Remi said.

"Is that code for 'Merrick, please call the hotel and extend our reservations?'"

Julien was watching her closely. She nodded to Merrick, who fished his phone out of his pocket. She hadn't planned on spending more than a weekend in Paris. Or more than ten minutes bothering Julien with this sordid horse racing business. But now...

You really don't have to leave me alone.

"Let's go into the office," Julien said, inclining his head to the door. He was slightly blushing as well. "We can talk there. Alone." He glanced at Salena, who waved her hand to shoo him from the room.

Remi followed Julien through the doorway. Behind her she heard Merrick flirting with Salena. Or attempting to.

"You married?" Merrick asked Salena.

"My family disowned me after I refused to submit to an arranged marriage," she said.

"Too bad. My family disowned me too," Merrick confessed.

"Did you also refuse a marriage?"

"No," he said. "I'm just an asshole."

"Merrick's an interesting guy," Julien said once they were out of earshot.

"He's obnoxious and weird. And he's flirting with your assistant."

"Salena's not my assistant."

"Girlfriend? I'll kill Merrick if you want me to. And even if you don't, I'll take any excuse at this point."

"Not my girlfriend, either. Long story." Julien pointed at an armchair. Remi glanced around. Julien had a lovely little office if rather cramped and messy. Only two chairs and a desk graced the room, which he'd decorated with old French cinema posters. He sat on a cushioned bench across from her, a curtained window behind him. "I'm guessing you didn't hire Merrick for his knowledge of Thoroughbreds."

"Or his charm. And not his face or body either, despite all the rumors about us. Most days I ask myself why I hired him. I haven't come up with a good answer yet. Although he helped me find you."

"Did he?"

"He's happy to do anything I ask him to do. Especially if it's immoral or unethical...like bribing a housekeeper for your address."

"Why did you want to find me? And will I

regret asking that question?" Julien grinned at her and she couldn't help but grin back. *Stop grinning like an idiot, Remi.* She was going to scare the boy if she didn't stop grinning.

"Probably," she admitted, forcing the smile off her face. This was business, not pleasure. "I'm here because something's rotten in the state of Kentucky. And I think our families might be involved."

CHAPTER THREE
ONE KISS, TWO KISS, RED KISS, BLUE KISS

Remi laid everything out for Julien as clearly and concisely as she could. His parents had just dropped ten million dollars on yearlings. Her parents suddenly had ten million dollars to blow on a five-hundred acre second farm. The private feud between the Capital Hill Brites and the Arden Farm Montgomerys had gone public this year, and it was the only story the racing press cared about. At the end of October, a Verona Downs Stakes race would take place. Six horses were entered. Shenanigans and Hijinks were the favorites. The feud and the Stakes race had even made the cover of Sports Illustrated. And creepy Tyson Balt had been at her parents' house and no one would talk about it.

"That doesn't sound good," Julien agreed.

"I don't know much about the farm, but I do know last winter Dad said they only had the funds for four million on yearlings."

"I triple-checked. They bought twenty-two yearlings for five million and then bought four broodmares and four stallions. In all, ten million dollars. And my parents paid cash for the farm—no mortgage. For four years, our little feud has been just between our families and anyone who was at the Christmas party at The Rails that night. Now it's all over the news. They act like we're the Hatfields and McCoys of horse racing."

"Did the article mention us specifically?" Julien asked.

"No, thank God," she said. "Although it's only a matter of time before the story comes out. The article just quotes a rumor that the feud started as a lovers' quarrel."

"They can't call it a lovers' quarrel if the two lovers didn't get to be lovers."

Remi grimaced. "Better than saying the manager of Arden Farms seduced the Brites' youngest son."

"I have a very old soul," he said. Remi laughed and buried her face in her hands. Between her fingers she peeked at him. He continued, "And my very old soul was dying to have sex with you that night."

"You're not making this any easier," she told him, lowering her hands.

"Can't help it. I'd rather talk about us than whatever our parents are into."

"Us?"

"Well...you know. What happened between us, I mean."

"Yeah, I'm sorry about that. I should have said that a long time ago."

"Don't be sorry. I'm not."

"I'm glad to hear that. I was worried you might be pissed I just showed up at your door almost four years later asking for help."

"I'll help you any way I can, Remi. It's just...it's really good to see you again."

Remi felt the heat in her face again. "You too, Julien."

They stared at each other until the silence grew heavy and awkward.

"Anyway," she said and wrenched her eyes away from him. "Sorry to be the bearer of this shitty news."

"It's okay, I promise. I wish I could help you. I'm happy to dig around a little if I can, talk to my sisters, see if they think something weird is going on. If my parents are doing something unethical, I'd rather find out from you than from the newspapers."

"Thank you. I hate to ask you to spy on your own family."

"I haven't exactly been thrilled with my parents recently either." Julien pulled his knee to his chest and wrapped his arm around his shin—the same arms that had once been wrapped around her.

"You moved across the ocean," she said. "That's not a great sign."

"They were asking for it," Julien said. "Two years ago when you got your promotion to farm manager, Mom said it was nepotism at its worst, that no way were you qualified to run Arden and the place would fall apart in a week. When Arden had its best season ever, Mom said it was un-ladylike for a woman to run a horse farm. Then it was the rants about how disgusting and disgraceful it was you had an 'attractive male assistant' you were obviously sleeping with. That's when Salena and I started packing."

"You moved out because your mother thought Merrick and I were sleeping together?" Remi asked, astounded Julien would still care about her after all this time.

"My issues with my parents are yet another really long story. Let's just say it was the last straw. Salena suggested we sublet a place in France for a few months. She used to live in Paris and knew I'd like it. I'm starting college again in January so I told my parents I was getting a little place in Paris until I started school."

"Not so little," she said, glancing around what she hoped was a two-bedroom apartment. "Although I can't imagine your parents or your sisters living in a three-floor walk-up garret apartment. No offense."

"None taken," Julien said, clearly finding the idea as amusing as she did. "But, for all its downsides, this place has one very big upside."

Julien turned around and opened the curtain behind him that shielded the window.

"Holy..." Remi rose out of her seat and walked to the window. Julien moved to the side and Remi sat next to him on the bench.

Through a gap in the buildings she could see the Eiffel Tower in all its illuminated nighttime glory. She stared at it in silence and sensed Julien's eyes on her, not the tower in the distance. Four years evaporated in an instant. Four years ago they were talking by the fireplace and now a window overlooking Paris. Four years come and gone in an instant.

"I used to dream about living in Paris," she said after a long pause. She couldn't quite believe that she was here in Paris with Julien Brite gazing at the Eiffel Tower. It was perfect —the cool of the city pressing against the window, the lights dancing on the tower, Julien at her side looking at her and nothing else. Not just perfect but a perfect moment—why did she keep having these with him? "When I was a little girl. Too many Madeline books, I guess."

"Who?"

"It's a girl thing." Remi gazed at the top of the tower, wondering what the city looked like from the top. Maybe she would see it before they left. Maybe Julien could take her there tomorrow.

"What did you dream about?" Julien asked, his voice low as if the entire city were trying to listen in, but he wanted to keep their conversation between only them.

"Oh, the usual kid dreams. Living in Paris, speaking French, eating croissants all the time."

"They are pretty amazing here," Julien agreed.

"Then I got older, and I still dreamed of Paris. When I was a teenager it seemed like the most romantic place in the world. I wanted to get my first kiss in Paris. Which, sadly, did not happen."

"Where did you get your first kiss?"

"In the Kentucky Theater in Lexington. Not nearly as romantic as Paris. You?"

"Um...the capital building actually. School field trip. Some girl in my class thought it would be rebellious to make out in the capital rotunda. The statue of Abraham Lincoln was watching us. Not romantic. A first kiss in Paris with the Eiffel Tower watching us would have been much better."

"Definitely," she said, smiling. When she turned her eyes back to Julien, she found him still looking at her. He wasn't smiling but the look on his face was better than a smile.

"Can I tell you something crazy?" she asked.

"Please. The crazier the better."

"I look for you at every race," she confessed. "Every single one of them. Kentucky. California. New York. Florida. Doesn't matter what the race is, what track we're at, I always look for your face in the crowd. You'd think after all this time I would quit looking for you. Is that crazy?"

He shook his head. "Not as crazy as me

writing you letters that I've never worked up the courage to send."

"Letters?"

"Real ones. Ink on paper."

"Why did you never send them?" she asked, hoping he still had the letters. "I wanted to write you too, or call you, or anything. But I was the older one and my parents forbade me from contacting you at all in case your parents got cops and lawyers involved."

"I didn't send them because I didn't think you'd want to read them." Julien took a heavy breath. "I convinced myself I was just a stupid lovestruck kid and no way would this beautiful older woman want to hear from me. Especially with everything that had happened."

"I would have loved to have heard from you, I promise. Even if it was just to tell me you were okay. I worried about you after that night."

"You did? Why?"

"I don't know. Just a feeling I had. I couldn't shake it. I saw your sisters at the races but never you. It was like you disappeared after Christmas. Maybe that's why I kept looking for you at every race I went to. Or maybe I just really like your face."

She raised her hand and stroked his cheek.

His skin felt warm—not feverish, simply heated. If he touched her face right now he too would feel her raised temperature just from the proximity of their bodies. She lowered her hand, afraid to touch him any further.

"That night at the party," Julien said, "I thought you were the most beautiful woman I'd ever seen in my life. How is it possible you're even more beautiful now?"

She knew she should say something, anything to dispel the anticipation, the tension that buzzed in the air between them. Their families were in a very public feud. Their families weren't just families but businesses. Getting involved with Julien could lead to accusations of collusion. Real ugly consequences. She needed to take a step back from Julien. Maybe two. Three would be best. Actually she should get on a plane and head straight for Kentucky.

Right now.

She kissed him.

Julien didn't seem the least surprised she kissed him. When their lips met he opened his mouth and let his tongue graze her tongue. She felt the kiss all the way from her lips to her toes and back up again.

Remi pulled away before the kiss turned

into more than a kiss. She'd been down that dangerous road before.

"I didn't mean to do that," Remi said.

"You didn't?" Julien asked, looking flushed and bright-eyed.

"No. Really. I was thinking in my head all the reasons I shouldn't kiss you and then..."

"I was thinking the same thing," he said. "Thinking that our parents' worst nightmare would be you and I getting involved and so we should absolutely not get involved."

"You're right. You're completely right."

"But I'm going to kiss you anyway," Julien said.

"Thank God."

He cupped the back of her neck and brought his mouth to hers. The second kiss was even more passionate than the first.

Julien kissed her like he'd die if he didn't, like he hadn't been kissed in a decade, like he had a gun to the back of his head and had been ordered to her kiss her like his life depended on it.

She wrapped her arms around his shoulders and pushed her breasts against his chest. She dug her fingers into the back of his hair and found it silky and soft. Julien's hand was on her thigh over her skirt, creating a thousand wicked images in her head. He could lift her skirt, pull off her panties, and bury himself inside her right now. And they could do it and she wouldn't feel at all guilty about it because he wasn't in high school anymore and his parents were across an ocean.

They paused in the kiss long enough to look at each other as if for confirmation that they could and would continue. In the distance, the lights on the Eiffel Tower turned to blue. And in the haze of blue light their lips met again.

Julien ran his hand down the center of her back. Remi held him even closer, tighter to her body.

This was crazy. This was wrong.

Those words bounced around her brain as they kissed but they stayed in her mind, unspoken. Yes, it was crazy. Yes, it was wrong. And no, that wasn't about to stop her.

She stopped only long enough to take a breath.

The Eiffel Tower turned red.

"What on earth?"

"Light show," Julien said. "They do it every night. But we can pretend it's just for us if you want."

"I want. God, I want."

She wanted to kiss him again and so she did. Or perhaps he kissed her this time. What did it matter who kissed whom as long as the kiss never ever ended? For four years they'd had this unfinished business hanging between them. Maybe they should finish it.

"I missed you," Julien said against her lips. "I kept trying to forget you, and I couldn't."

"I think of you every Christmas," she whispered back. "Christmas hasn't been the same since that night. No matter what I get it's never what I want."

"What do you want?" Julien asked and she knew he wasn't asking about Christmas gifts.

"Another Christmas with you," she whispered.

"You can have that," he said. "And me if you want."

She rested her forehead against his. One minute. That's all she needed was one minute of not kissing to clear her head so she could think straight. Remi took a deep breath.

"Julien, if we get involved, our parents are going to kill us," she said. "I'm not saying we shouldn't get involved. I'm saying there will be consequences."

"My mother thinks it's shameful Arden

Farms has a female manager. My father routinely calls you a slut. And your family and my family are somehow making millions of dollars off a staged horse rivalry. You think I care what they think?"

"Yes," she said. "Same way I care about what my parents think, because they love me and I love them even if they are pissing me the hell off right now."

"I care too," he admitted. "But not enough to stop kissing you."

"No more kissing until we get back to your bedroom. You kiss me again like that, and we'll never make it back."

"Kiss you like what?" he asked as he half-dragged her off of the bench.

"Kiss me like you haven't kissed anybody in a really long time and you need to make up for lost time."

"Would it completely freak you out if I told you that was true?"

"No, of course not. We all have dry spells."

"This is a little more than a dry spell," Julien said, looking sheepish. She knew that look. Julien had worn that same expression right before confessing he was only seventeen.

"What is it? You can tell me."

"That's kind of a long story."

"You have a lot of long stories. You ran away from Kentucky and moved to Paris to get away from your parents who were mean to me. You have an assistant who isn't your assistant but who lives with you. And you've had more than a dry spell? What's going on? Tell me."

He winced, then said, "Dry spell is an understatement."

"Oh shit." Remi covered her mouth with her hand.

"Don't ask," he said, a look of quiet desperation in his eyes. "Please."

"Oh my God."

"I have a good excuse, I swear."

"You're a virgin?" she asked, utterly astounded.

"I asked you not to ask." Julien crossed his arms over his chest and laughed nervously.

"I'm sorry."

"Does it really bother you?"

"I'm just shocked," Remi said, looking at Julien in a new light.

"Shocked?"

"You're beautiful, Julien. I thought that the second I saw you four years ago. I thought that the second I saw you again tonight. And now you're blushing, and you're even sexier than you were four seconds before."

"Let's go talk in my room. There's something I need to tell you. And show you."

"Your naked body?"

"That too."

They left his office and paused in the now empty living room.

"Wonder where Merrick and Salena went?" Julien whispered.

"It's Merrick. Five bucks says they're in her bedroom."

Julien looked skeptical. "Salena's really picky about the guys she dates."

"It's Merrick. Trust me, this isn't about dating."

Julien took her hand and they crept past a closed door. They heard a voice from within.

"So how old are you?" they heard Merrick saying.

"Thirty-three. You?" Salena asked.

"Thirty-six. You put us together and you get sixty-nine."

'You're very good at math."

"Who was doing math?" Merrick asked.

"Mystery solved," Julien whispered and rolled his eyes. He looked so cute with his amused disgust that Remi had to stop herself from grabbing his face and kissing him again. "Let's go."

They quickly reached his room at the end of his hall. He pushed the door open and ripped a small folded piece of paper off the door. He glanced at the note, smiled, and shoved it into his pocket. As soon as they were in the room with the door locked behind them, Julien pulled her to him. Remi raised her hand and covered his mouth.

"No kissing. You talk to me first," she said.

"My man't malk wiff your mand on my mouth."

"What?" she asked, pulling her hand back.

"I can't talk with your hand on my mouth," Julien said.

"Okay, you talk. I'll be sitting at a safe distance and listening." Remi picked up a chair and sat it five feet from the bed where Julien now sat. She was impressed by his bedroom. The walls were an elegant jade green and the bedframe an antique brass. The walls were lined with beautiful, if bizarre art, and every surface was spotlessly clean.

"Wow. Your room is really clean," she said. "That's not natural."

"Salena hired a housekeeper. Was not my idea. I'm not that spoiled."

"I want to know about Salena. She's way too beautiful, she lives with you, but she's not your assistant."

"And she's seen me naked. A lot. Just making sure you know everything."

"I really hope there's a good explanation for that." Remi wasn't the jealous type, but she was quickly getting used to the idea of being the only woman who got to see Julien naked.

"There is. And it has everything to do with why, I'm, you know..."

"Undefiled?"

"That's a diplomatic word for a guy who's never gotten laid."

"I'm trying to be diplomatic. It's better than ripping your clothes off," Remi said, and sat on her hands to remind herself to let him talk before the clothes-ripping began.

"I think I'd rather you just rip my clothes off."

"Talk," she ordered.

"Okay, I'm talking. It's just...I don't talk about this often. It sort of changes everything when I bring it up."

"Bring what up? What is it?"

"The reason I'm a virgin and the reason Salena lives with me and the reason I have a housekeeper who keeps everything spotless and disinfected and the reason I lived with my parents until last year until I finally couldn't stand it anymore and the reason I didn't send you all the letters I wrote you..."

"What's the reason?"

Julien took a deep breath. He seemed to be steeling himself. "Salena's not my assistant, but she does work for us."

"What does she do?"

"She's my doctor. Dr. Salena Kar. Internist."

Remi's mouth fell open. She quickly closed it. Her desire for Julien turned instantly to pity, compassion, and fear.

"You have a live-in doctor?" she whispered.

"I do."

"What do you have?"

Julien sighed again. "It's not what I have. It's what I had."

"Which was?"

"Leukemia, Remi. Two weeks after you and I almost had sex, I was diagnosed with leukemia."

CHAPTER FOUR

"Leukemia," Remi repeated. Her mouth formed the word but her tongue wanted to spit it back out, reject the word, the truth, the suffering Julien had experienced.

"Acute myeloid leukemia, if you want to be specific."

"That sounds...bad."

Julien laughed a little. "There's no good leukemia."

"No," Remi breathed, her hands shaking from the shock of the news. "I wouldn't think so. What happened?"

Julien shrugged and sighed. She knew he didn't want to tell the story but she had to hear it. Every word.

"The night of the Christmas party, you thought I was older than I was. Why?"

"I don't know," she said. "You were almost six feet tall and had a glass of wine in your hand."

"I thought it was probably the wine that made you think I was older."

"That and how intelligent and funny you were. I'm surprised your parents let you drink wine."

"They usually didn't. But I had a headache that day. It got worse at the party. Dad said I could have one glass of wine and if that didn't help I should just go lie down in one of the guest bedrooms. They'd find me when it was time to go. That's why Mom was looking for me."

"You didn't tell me you had a headache that night."

"I'd had a headache off and on for a week. When I saw you and we started talking, it disappeared. But it came back the next day. A week after Christmas, I started getting bruises. They wouldn't heal. I finally told Mom I thought something was wrong with me, and I showed her the bruises on my stomach. Next day I'm in the doctor's office getting blood drawn and my mom's crying and the doctor's looking at my blood in the tube and scowling."

"Scowling is not good," Remi said, her

hands shaking as if it had been her in that room next to Julien watching a doctor stick a needle in his arm.

"The doctor said he was going to run some tests, and I should pray I got an A on the tests."

"An A?"

"A is for 'anemia,' which is easy to treat and would have explained the bruises and the headaches. I got a C on my test instead. Cancer. They admitted me into the hospital immediately. Then home for a few days. Then I was back in the hospital again. After the bone marrow transplant, I pretty much lived in the hospital."

"How bad was it?"

"Bad," he said simply. "But it's always bad. With cancer it's either bad or worse. Mine was bad, so it could have been worse. That's what you tell yourself to make it through the night. Mine was treatable, even curable. Not all of the big C's are."

Her heart ground against the gears of her chest. Julien spoke of his years facing death so casually, too casually.

"So you're better? Completely?"

"See that?" Julien pointed to a chart on the wall. "That's a five-year calendar. Declared in total remission one year and eleven months ago. That's when the countdown starts. At five years if I'm still clear, then I'm cured. But the likelihood of relapse is extremely low at this point."

"Good," she said, giving him a shaky smile. "That's good."

"But you should know, there are some lingering issues. I'd get Salena in here to tell you all the dirty details, but I think she's a little busy right now."

Remi stood up and walked over to his bed. She touched the side of his face. "I want *you* to tell me, no one else."

He shrugged and rolled onto his back. Not able to stay away from him any longer, she stretched out on her side next to him. Julien stared up at the ceiling.

"Okay, dirty details. Leukemia sucks. I lived in the hospital for months at a time. Radiation makes you skeletal. No teenage guy wants to weigh ninety pounds. Then you get chemo and steroids and you blow up like a balloon. There are literally zero pictures of me from age seventeen to nineteen in existence. Skeletal. Fat. Skeletal. Fat. I banned cameras."

"I was wondering why I never found any

pictures of you. Your family's in the news all the time."

"Even when I was having good days, feeling okay, Mom wouldn't let me out of the house. All the treatments kill the immune system."

"House arrest?"

"Basically," Julien said. "Which was okay at first. Mom and Dad never talked about me being sick to anyone. I asked them not to, and they respected that."

"You were sick. That's nothing to be embarrassed about."

"I know that now. Harder to accept when you're seventeen and bald and there are days you can't even go to the bathroom without help. I didn't want visitors. I didn't want people all over me. I just wanted to get through it and get on with my life."

"I can see that, but still... God, if I'd known you were sick, I would never have let my family say a word about your family even around our kitchen table. This stupid feud would have been over even if I had to tie up, gag, and chain every last relative and throw them in the basement."

"Kinky," Julien said. Remi flicked him in the arm. "Sorry."

"Don't be," Remi said. "Just keep talking. I want to know everything."

"This next part is kind of embarrassing."

"Tell me, Julien. Please tell me everything."

"I'm sterile," Julien said. He glanced her way before staring assiduously at the ceiling again.

"You mean, *sterile* sterile?"

"Chemotherapy plus bone marrow transplant means goodbye to your fertility forever. It's possible I could have kids someday. They froze some of my sperm."

"That was smart."

"Smart and horrible. Talk about humiliating, sitting in front of your doctor with your mom next to you and discussing your sperm."

"Oh God, you poor thing." Remi could have cried at the thought of what Julien had endured. She felt an ache, almost physical, to go back in time and somehow be there for him and with him while he'd gone through it all.

"Yeah, that was a bad day." He laughed softly and rubbed his forehead. "I don't think Mom's ever recovered from the 'Save Julien's sperm' conversation either. Anyway, thought you should know that part up front."

"As long as I have my horses and my

horses have babies, I don't need much else," she said before realizing they were already talking about the future. Where had this come from? She didn't know. Right now she didn't care. "That doesn't bother me."

"Seriously?"

"Seriously. Anything else I need to know?" she asked.

"Nothing much more to tell. Oh, except this. Two years after diagnosis I'm finally in remission. After about six months after that I started to feel pretty normal. I looked normal too. My hair was back. It was short but at least I had some. I couldn't wait to get out of the house. I was starting college and was so ready to have a girlfriend."

"And have sex?" she teased.

"All the sex," he said.

"So what happened?"

"My immune system still wasn't one hundred percent. I caught a cold. The cold turned into pneumonia. I had to take a medical leave from school two months in. I've never been back to school. College drop-out. Thank God for trust funds, right?"

"Why didn't you go back to school when you were better?"

"Mom took the pneumonia as a sign I

should be in lockdown. Do you know how hard it is to meet women when your mother won't let you out of your own house?"

"Pretty damn hard, I'd guess," Remi said as she laid her hand on his chest. They'd been making out in his office a half hour ago. Surely touching him wouldn't be presumptuous. Clearly it wasn't, as Julien placed his hand over her hand.

"And it's really hard to kiss someone when you're under orders to wear a surgical mask."

"You had to wear surgical masks?"

"Everyone in the house wore them around me," Julien said. "And that's where Salena comes in. My parents hired Salena to be my live-in doctor. She had burn-out and student loans from med school. My parents paid off her loans, and now she has only the one patient. Well, two patients counting Mom. First thing Salena did was diagnose my mother with 'Vulnerable Child Syndrome.' Real syndrome. It's basically, pathological overprotectiveness. And then she wrote her a prescription. Four words: 'Let Julien move out.'"

Remi would have applauded if her hand had been free. "Thank God for Salena. That's really smart, writing it on a prescription pad."

"Doctor's orders," Julien said. "Salena

writes me prescriptions all the time. 'Go running' or 'Go hiking' or 'Ask her out on a date.'"

"She writes you prescriptions for dates?"

"I know. She's awesome, right? I had to have a ton of tests and stuff to get cleared to have sex. You know, they had to make sure my immune system could take it. Salena did all the tests and then after I got cleared, she sat me in her office and gave me a three-hour lecture on sex, women, and the female anatomy. She had charts and diagrams. The films were my favorite part. It was amazing. I've never had sex, but I know where the clitoris and the g-spot are, and I know what to do when I find them."

"Can I go kiss Salena now? On the mouth?"

"Can I watch?" Julien asked.

"Of course."

"I love Salena," Julien said with a wide-eyed exhalation. "She's my hero and my best friend. She rescued me from my own house, makes me go out, have a life, try new things."

"Like moving to Paris?"

"Once I was cleared for 'adult activities' as Salena calls them, she staged an intervention with my parents and told them they were making things worse by keeping me cooped up and treating me like I was on death's doorstep. My parents worship doctors so they took her seriously and let me go. I just had to take Salena with me so she could monitor my medical condition."

"So you ran off to Paris?"

"I said Paris. They assumed Paris, Kentucky. I didn't exactly correct them."

"Did they freak out?" Remi asked.

"They did at first. But Salena talked sense into them. France has the best health care system in the world. Much better than the States. And I'm healthy as a horse now. Salena makes sure of that."

"I'm happy to hear that." Remi realized she might have made the understatement of the century with that statement. "Ecstatic" would have been more accurate.

"My parents are calmer now about the Paris thing. Salena loves it here. I love it here. Been learning the language, trying to meet people."

"Meet women?"

Julien shrugged. "Been on a few dates."

"Only a few?"

Julien gave her a crooked smile and a half-hearted chuckle.

"Did you know 'cancer' is the same word

in English and in French? No matter what language, the word sends girls running. It's not that it's in the past. That's not what scares people. It's that it can come back. It might come back. Anytime I get a headache, a cold, anything, my family freaks out. Anybody who is in my life will share in that fear. Hard to ask that much courage from someone you just met, right? No wonder the girls go running when I tell them the truth."

Remi rose up and looked down at Julien still lying on his back on the bed.

"I'm not running," she said.

"Why not?" Julien asked.

"I am the least romantic person I've ever known," she confessed. "But for some reason..."

She said no more because she knew she didn't have to.

"I know," Julien said in a low voice, almost scared.

"I've never forgotten you. I should have. I was a senior in college. I should have gotten over you a long time ago. I never did. And now that I'm here with you, I feel like this is exactly where I'm supposed to be."

"Although it ended badly, I was so grateful we had that night at the Christmas party.

When I was alone in the hospital, sick and scared and I thought maybe I would just stop fighting, go to sleep and never wake up again... I would think of that night with you. I remembered kissing you, touching you, being touched by you, and it helped me remember what I was fighting for. A future where I was healthy again and wasn't alone. You were with me the whole time, Remi."

Remi blinked back tears. Neither of them spoke. A heavy, meaningful silence descended. She didn't want to rush things, didn't want to push him. But for all her noble intentions, she also wanted to kiss him again, touch every inch of him, and spend all night with him in this bed helping him make up for lost time and show him exactly what he'd been fighting for.

"This is going to sound like a line," Julien finally said, "but I swear it isn't. The thing is... when you spend age seventeen to nineteen thinking you might die, it changes the way you look at your life. I decided I wanted to move to Paris on a Thursday. Salena and I were on a plane Monday. When you want to do something, you do it. You don't wait a week, a year. Because you know you might not be around next year, next week."

"*Carpe diem*?" Remi asked.

"That means 'seize the day,'" Julien said. "It's night."

"*Carpe*... Hold on a second. Merrick?" she called out loudly, loud enough she knew her voice carried throughout the entire apartment.

"Little busy, Boss!" he yelled back, his voice easily penetrating the wall of Julien's bedroom.

"What's Latin for 'night'?"

"Depends on the part of speech!"

"Direct object!"

"*Noctem!*" he yelled.

"Thank you!"

"*Carpe noctem*," Remi whispered to Julien although seconds earlier she'd been shouting at Merrick. "Seize the night."

"We could have just Googled that," Julien said.

"I know. But I wanted a little payback for all the times Merrick starts conversations with me when I'm in the bathroom. Plus, what's the point in having a genius assistant who knows Latin without asking him to help you with your Latin?"

"Good point."

"So..." Remi said as that tense, taut silence descended on the room again.

Remi slid her hand up and down the center of Julien's chest. With each pass down his stomach she moved lower. Under her hand she felt his stomach fluttering. Julien was nervous. She liked that.

"So..." Julien said. "What do you want to do?"

"It's your decision," she said. "You have more to lose than I do."

Julien laughed and his stomach muscles dance under her hand. "Literally," he said.

"How about this? How about I kiss you right now and you kiss me back, and we'll keep kissing until something more happens or we fall asleep?"

"I like that idea. And, you know, *carpe noctem.*"

She nodded and whispered. "*Seize the night.*"

Remi leaned over Julien and brought her lips to his.

Julien slid his fingers through her hair and pulled her even closer as the kiss deepened. The position was uncomfortable enough Remi felt entirely justified in yanking her skirt to her knees and straddling Julien's thighs. Julien inhaled sharply.

"I don't weigh too much, do I?" Remi

asked, freezing. At five-nine with muscles and curves, she possibly weighed more than Julien.

"You weigh the perfect amount and the perfect amount of you sort of came in contact with a certain part of me. Please do it again."

Remi laughed and settled in on top of him. The kissing, at first tentative, quickly turned torrid. Julien might not have done much kissing in his life, but Remi had no complaints about his technique. She couldn't get enough of his mouth, nor he hers. Julien rolled them onto their sides without breaking the kiss. He slipped his hand under her shirt and caressed her back. She wanted to feel his skin too, as much of it as she could. She slid her hand under his t-shirt and rubbed his side. He was so warm and young and eager, she knew if he wanted, kissing would only be the beginning of their night together.

"You smell like roses," Julien whispered into her neck as he nibbled under her ear.

"It's my soap."

"It's not your soap, it's your skin. It's all of you,," he said, his hand now at the center of her back, teasing the expanse between her shoulder blades.

"If you're trying to seduce me, it's working." Remi pushed her hips into his. Pressure was already starting to build inside her.

"I thought you were trying to seduce me?" Julien teased.

"I can if you want me to."

"I'd love to see you try," he said, a wicked grin on his face. She adored that face, adored those eyes that shone so bright with desire.

"Let's see, when we were last alone together in a bedroom, I believe I was..."

She came up on her knees and unbuttoned her blouse. Julien reached out and helped pull her shirt down her arms. She threw it onto the floor with a flourish. Julien knelt in front of her and kissed the tops of her breasts. She forced herself to do nothing as he kissed her neck and chest. They shouldn't rush things. This night could be Julien's first time. He'd spent his teen years fighting for his life. Why not show him exactly how much light had been waiting for him at the end of that tunnel?

"You're really okay, now?" Remi asked as Julien wrapped his arms around her back and pulled her even closer. They faced each other on their knees, her breasts pressing against his chest. She could feel his heart pounding.

"I'm fine. You're not going to hurt me, I promise."

"Good," she said and pushed him down onto his back. He laughed as she straddled him again. But the laughter stopped the moment she unhooked her bra and took it off. She took him by his wrists and brought his hands to her breasts.

"Oh my God," he said, holding her breasts, squeezing and cupping them. "I've missed them so much."

Remi laughed but the laugh abruptly turned to a gasp when Julien pinched her nipples. A shock of pleasure bolted through her from her breasts to her back and all the way down her spine. Her nipples hardened as Julien teased them and gently tugged them. She closed her eyes and did nothing but let him touch her. She felt his erection pressing against her even through his jeans.

"Your turn," she said breathlessly. "I don't want to be the only shirtless person in the room."

"Okay, but..."

She shook her head. "No butts yet. Just your shirt."

Remi sat back so Julien could roll up. He

sighed heavily before pulling his shirt off over his head.

"It's not as bad as it looks," he said, lying on his back again.

Remi gazed down at his chest. He was thin, yes. Thin but muscular. He'd clearly taken getting into shape after his recovery very seriously. He had a chiseled stomach, sinewy biceps, a broad chest, and...

"No," she said. "It's not bad at all."

She reached out and touched the raised four-inch scar on the right-hand side of his upper chest. It was smooth and bright pink, much like Julien's face at the moment.

"They put this thing in your chest—a mediport," he explained. "It's how the drugs are delivered."

"Then I'm glad you have the scar. It saved your life."

"The day they took it out was the best day of my life. Until today."

Remi's fingers fluttered. When had she ever desired someone this much?

"It's hideous I know," Julien said, wincing slightly.

"It's not bad at all."

"Good. You can keep staring at it. It'll give me an excuse to stare at your, you know."

"Boobs? Breasts? Tits?"

"All of the above..."

Remi put her hands on either side of his shoulders and lay on top of him. When her bare breasts touched his naked chest, he inhaled sharply.

"You okay?" she asked.

"I'm so happy I'm not dead right now, I could cry," he said. "Am I dead? Is this heaven? Can you get massive hardons in heaven?"

"Wouldn't be heaven otherwise." Remi rolled onto her side so Julien could have total access to her chest. They lay face-to-face, kissing as he ran his hand over both her breasts, gently touching, squeezing, holding, caressing. He lightly pinched her nipples between his thumb and forefinger. His touch gave her breathtaking amounts of pleasure. As he touched her, she slid her hand up and down his arm, relishing the ridges of muscle he'd worked so hard for after recovering.

Remi threw her leg over Julien's hip to bring his body even closer to hers.

He closed his eyes tight as if he were in pain. "I am seriously turned on right now," he said. "Sorry."

"Don't say you're sorry. Do you want to stop or keep going?"

"Keep going. Definitely."

"Are you saying that because you mean it or because you're turned on?"

"Both is my answer," he said. "If that's the right answer."

"There is no right or wrong answer. It's whatever you want," she said, running her hand through his hair again and stroking the side of his face.

"I want you." Julien took her chin in his hand and caressed her bottom lip with his thumb. "I want you so much it hurts. But..."

"I know," she said. "If our families find out about this, we're dead."

"Very dead. And me and death were on speaking terms not that long ago. I know death. They'll kill us."

"Whatever they're up to, they need the press to think both families hate each other." Remi knew this public rivalry was making them all a fortune.

"And they do hate each other," Julien said. "They just love money more."

"So what do we do?" Remi asked, aching at the thought of walking away from Julien so soon after finding him. "We can't just pretend I'm not a Montgomery and you're not a Brite."

"Maybe we can for one night," he said. "You're just Remi. I'm just Julien. No last names."

Remi grinned at him. Not a bad idea. Whatever they did tonight was no one's business but theirs. Why should it matter what their last names were? It shouldn't, obviously. That was the answer. Now that she had that answer, she had only one question.

"Okay, Just-Julien, now what do you want to do?"

Now what do you want to do? Remi had asked Julien, and he hesitated before answering.

"Maybe we should follow the doctor's orders," Julien said with a sly smile.

"Doctor's orders?" Remi asked.

Julien pulled the paper out of his pocket that had been taped to the door. He unfolded it and showed it to her. It was a prescription pad for Dr. Salena Kar. And the good Dr. Kar had prescribed a very special medicine for Julian.

S-E-X, it read in all caps. The one and only word on it.

"Well, she *is* the doctor," Remi said.

Julian threw the note in the air and wrapped both arms around Remi. He pressed

Remi back onto the bed, and lightly gripped her wrists. He kissed her from her neck to her breasts and drew a nipple into his mouth and sucked it gently.

"That is such a good idea, Just-Julien," she sighed with relief, his choice made. He wanted her as much as she wanted him. "Whoever you are."

"I'm nobody," he whispered against her skin. "I'm just a random guy you met in Paris."

"I was here for a vacation," she said as he kissed his way across her chest to her other nipple. "I work my ass off."

"You needed a vacation," Julien said. "And I needed your ass." He playfully cupped her bottom and squeezed.

"I did. And while on vacation I saw a gorgeous younger man walking down the street."

"How gorgeous?"

"Beyond gorgeous. Striking. Not normal gorgeous. Different. Big black eyes—"

"Did someone punch him, you think?" Julien looked up at her and winked.

"Someone's going to if he doesn't get back to her nipples," she teased.

Julien laughed before taking her nipple into his mouth again. She moaned as the heat seeped into her skin and sent delicious shivers all the way to the pit of her stomach. Her clitoris was swelling. She couldn't stop her hips from moving against Julien.

"So what else about this guy?" Julien asked as he palmed her breast.

"I'm not sure. I feel like I've known him all my life. Usually I don't jump into bed this fast with a guy but he seems special. And not just because of the aforementioned striking-ness."

"Is that a word?"

"It is now. But I think maybe this is something...I don't know."

"I know," Julien said, looking up at her. "I feel it too. Like this was meant to happen, and we have to let it happen."

"Do you want it to happen?" she asked.

Julien nodded.

"Then we'll let it happen," she said, her voice as soft and tender as the look on Julien's face. And she knew they weren't talking about sex anymore. Not only sex anyway. But them. The future. Whatever it meant. They would let it happen. Their hearts left them no other choice.

No more words were exchanged. No more words were needed. Julien stood up and Remi pulled the covers back on the bed. She rested on her back, propped on her elbows and watched Julien undress. He didn't hesitate, not even when the moment came to take his boxer briefs off.

He had a beautiful young body and she devoured the sight of it. Once Julien was naked, she unzipped her skirt in the back. Julien pulled it down her legs and tossed it to the floor. She had on nothing but her panties now. Julien crawled onto the bed and stretched out on top of her.

Remi reached between their bodies and wrapped her hand around his erection. She stroked upward as Julien closed his eyes.

"I remember that," he said as she ran her fingers from the wet tip to the base and back up again. She touched him lightly at first and then gripped him firmly with her entire hand.

"You remember me touching you like this?"

"It's better than I remembered, Remi. It's better than I dreamed. And I dreamed this moment so many times."

His eyes were closed and soft breaths escaped his slightly parted lips.

"Tell me what you dreamed," she said, gently rubbing the tip until she felt wetness.

"What I dreamed?"

"When I was a teenager, I used to dream

about what my first time would be like. I was young and romantic and wanted my first time to be beautiful and special. But then I had a boring first time with a boring guy, because I was nineteen and I couldn't wait any longer. But you had to wait. And now it's time. So tell me how you wanted it, how you dreamed of it happening, and maybe we can make your dream come true," she said.

"Remi..."

"Tell me please," she said. "Let me do this for you."

Julien exhaled and opened his eyes. "I had a ton of fantasies. They were great distractions from real life. Real life sucked for a long time."

"How did you want it to happen?"

"In my bed," he said. "No fancy hotels, no castles or anything. When you're in the hospital, your own bed becomes this symbol—home. Not just home but home-free. When they let you go home for good, it's because you're better. So being in my own bed at home would mean I was good, out of the woods. And that was a very sexy thought."

"Here we are, in your own bed. Anything else?" she asked as she kissed his neck.

"I liked the thought of being on my back for the first time. But when you're seventeen all you want to do is see breasts. Everywhere. All the time."

"That can be arranged," she said. "What else?"

"I dreamed..." He paused. "This is stupid."

"Tell me anyway."

"I dreamed that my first time would be with someone who was really happy to be my first time. And second. And third."

"It's a good dream," she said, running a hand down the center of his back. "I'm thrilled to be your first time and can't wait for the second and third. So let's make your dream come true."

Remi held her breath as Julien eased her panties down her legs. She was nervous which made no sense. He was the virgin, not her. But that was the reason, the one remaining rational part of her brain told her. She was nervous for Julien. She wanted him to enjoy every second of his first time. After all he'd been through, after what he'd survived, she wanted his first time to be perfect.

She kicked her underwear off her ankle and opened her legs for him. He slid his hand up her thigh as he looked at her. The only light in the room came from the bedside lamp and the streetlights streaming in through the window. But it was light enough for him to see every part of her.

"Good? Bad? Weird?" she asked, as he traced the seam of her labia with his fingertip.

"Amazing," he breathed. Remi smiled and settled deep into his bed and let him touch her. First he caressed her outer lips with his fingertips. When she whispered a desperate "please, Julien" he pushed one finger inside her. He closed his eyes for a moment as if wanting to focus solely on his sense of touch. "You're so wet inside. And warm."

"I'm turned on. That's what happens to women when we get turned on."

He grinned. "I know. Doctor Salena gave me the lowdown on your down-lows."

"My down-lows are grateful."

"God, you feel so good. I want you turned on like this all the time forever and ever," he said, opening his eyes again.

"I don't think that'll be a problem if I'm around you."

He pushed in a second finger, and she sighed with pleasure and need. He went in deep and pulled out again, in and out, as she grew even wetter and hotter on the inside.

She opened her legs even wider and Julien

pushed in a third finger. Remi flinched with pleasure and Julien froze.

"Don't stop," she said. "Everything you're doing is good."

He nodded and pushed his three fingers into her again, in deep. She felt full and open, but not uncomfortably so. She wanted him to experience all of her, inside and out. He explored her with his fingertips, running them up and down the front wall. He hit a spot inside her, and Remi gasped loudly.

"Good?" he asked.

"Do it again," she begged.

"Yes, ma'am," he said, laughing. He massaged her g-spot, rubbing it with gentle spirals that sent Remi's hips lifting off the bed. She grabbed the brass bar of the headboard behind her. So much tension built in Remi that she had to breathe deeply and slowly to keep from coming right then and there on Julien's hand. It felt so good, but she wasn't ready for it to end yet. She'd had good sex before. Even great sex. But she'd never felt this open before, never been this wet and this aroused, and never wanted someone inside her so much in life.

"What do you want me to do?" Julien

asked, his voice as breathless as hers. "I want you to come."

"I'm really close," she panted.

"Tell me what you like," he said. "I'm supposed to ask that." He looked down at her with his dark eyes shining, his skin flushed, his lips wet and parted. She rose up and kissed him, needing to taste his mouth again.

She reached between her legs and pulled his hand out of her. With her hand over his hand she guided him to her clitoris.

"There," she said. "Kissing here or touching here is how the magic happens."

"I want to make the magic happen," he said, lightly gripping her clitoris between his thumb and forefinger.

"That..." Remi collapsed onto her back again, "is magical."

She could feel her clitoris swelling even more under his touch. Lost as she was in the ecstasy, she barely noticed him sliding down the bed until she felt his tongue on her. He pushed three fingers back into her as he sucked on the tight knot. Remi twined her fingers through his soft hair and held his neck gently as he pumped his fingers into her and licked her simultaneously. No amount of deep breathing could stop her from coming now. Her entire body went stiff and still for what felt like an eternity as Julien lapped at her with the hunger of a starving man.

With one hoarse cry, Remi came, her inner muscles fluttering hard and deep inside her, the muscles twitching around Julien's fingers, her clitoris throbbing against his tongue.

"Stop," she said and Julien immediately pulled his fingers from her and sat up.

"You okay?" He sounded almost scared.

"More than okay. I am incredible." She slowly opened her eyes.

"That was the sexiest thing ever," Julien said, cupping her breast with his wet fingers. Her nipples had grown more sensitive with arousal. The heat from his hand seeped deep into her skin. She never wanted him to stop touching her.

"It's not always easy to make a woman orgasm. You should be proud of yourself."

"I plan on doing it again as soon as you let me." Julien pinched her nipple and rolled it between his fingers.

"Your turn," she said, laying a hand on the side of his face. "Ready?"

Julien heaved a breath and she felt a slight tremor pass through his body. Her heart galloped inside her chest at the look of trust and need on his face. She pulled him close and kissed him again. She didn't have the words to tell him how much it meant to her that he wanted her to be his first, so she tried to tell him with the kiss.

Remi rolled him onto his back. She pushed her hips into his hips, sliding her wet and open body over his erection. The tip of his penis nudged the entrance of her vagina. Without breaking the kiss she pushed back. As wet as she was the tip slid right in. Julien raised his hips and inch-by-inch entered her completely.

Remi placed her hands on either side of Julien's shoulders and pulled back from this kiss. His eyes were closed, his lips slightly parted. She pushed against him again and his shoulders rolled off the bed.

"Remi," he panted. She'd never loved the sound of her name so much as when he said it.

"Hold my hips," she whispered, not wanting to break the spell of the moment.

He took her hips in his large strong hands and held them tight as she moved on him. She kept the pace slow and easy, letting Julien get used to being inside a woman before taking things further. Looking down, she saw where their bodies united and became one. Julien was looking too.

She took a deep breath. She would start slow with him, let him feel everything as she moved on him. His hands held her thighs, and she let him set the pace of her movements at first, the rhythm of their joining.

Joining...that was it. She couldn't think of what they did in this bed together as "fucking," even though she knew that's what the world would call it. She'd fucked him with her eyes the moment she'd seen him again for the first time in four years standing in his doorway. He'd fucked her with his fingers moments ago as she'd lay splayed open for him against his pillows. He'd fucked her with his mouth and now she fucked him for the first time in his short life that could have been so much shorter—a thought that terrified her so much her own terror terrified her. But it didn't feel like fucking to her even as the room grew warm from their bodies and sweat trickled down her back and his fingers smelled of her arousal and his mouth tasted of her desire. She licked it off his lips.

Joining was the word that echoed in her blood. For four years their two families had pushed apart from each other—a foolish drunken quarrel that forced everyone to pick a side and go to war. But here on these pale gold sheets where Julien Brite's body disappeared inside Remi Montgomery's, the fight they'd accidentally began one foolish night ended inside her.

Remi pressed her palms onto Julien's chest and drove her pelvis into his with concentrated effort, clenching her inner muscles tightly around him. She wanted him to feel everything as she rode him. His back bowed underneath her, his length deep in her, hot and hard. She ground into him, against him, on him with a renewed frenzy. Beneath her Julien gasped and breathed and gasped again. He'd lost control of himself too and nothing could stop him from lifting his hips in short hard pulses as if seeking to tunnel as far into Remi as possible.

Their bodies were slick with sweat. She could hear the wetness that sealed him to her with each movement. The heat grew almost unbearable. She felt lightheaded even as a heaviness settled into her lower body. Julien latched onto her right breast and sucked her nipple with desperate hunger. They had promised tonight last names would be banished. She was Just-Remi and he Just-Julien.

But in that moment when he was inside her vagina and she inside his mouth, they couldn't possibly be more joined to each other.

Julien's head fell back onto his pillow, his lower back arching off the bed as he came inside her, filling her up with his semen that shot into her, coating the walls that clasped him. As he came, Remi rode him into the bed with wild movements that brought her to the edge and left her hanging there. Julien emerged from his haze long enough to press two fingers into her clitoris so deep they almost slid inside her. The touch, rough but necessary, sent her falling over the edge. She collapsed onto his chest as her second climax shook her to the core.

Haltingly and carefully, they disentangled from each other. A sweet exhaustion suffused her entire being. She could do nothing but roll onto her back and let the night air cool her burning skin. Julien's wetness poured out of her, glazing her thighs and staining the sheets. She did the math and realized it was nearly six in the morning back in Kentucky. She wanted to stay up all night with Julien but her body wouldn't let her. There would be tomorrow, however, and then they could do this again and again and again.

Remi waited for Julien to speak, to laugh or sigh or to congratulate himself in some way for divesting himself of his virginity, and with an older woman too. It was what she'd expect from any young man who'd fought long and hard to experience a night like tonight. But he wasn't just any young man.

"We're going to get in huge trouble for this, aren't we?" Julien asked.

She smiled at the ceiling. In this torrid hour when he should have been thinking of sex and passion and conquest and everything that had happened and would no doubt happen again between them, instead he thought of her, of them, of what the future held, and what price they'd be asked to pay for what they'd done. Their families were very likely making a lot of money for stoking a very ugly rivalry in the press, and with one act, Remi and Julien had just merged the two families.

"With who?" she asked.

"Our—" he began and stopped. She heard his laugh, felt the bed move with it, then felt the bed move again as he lay on his side and rested his hand on her still quivering stomach.

"No one," he said. "No one at all."

Just-Remi fell asleep minutes later, her

back tucked against Just-Julien's chest. Far too soon she would be a Montgomery of Arden Farms again. Far too soon he would be a Brite of Capital Hills again. But tonight in this bed that bore the last remnants of his virginity, she took on another identity—the only one that mattered.

His.

Remi awoke with the first light and found Julien already awake and sitting by the window. He had something in his hands—a book or magazine. She couldn't tell. She looked at him sitting in the sunlight. In the glint of the morning she could see every inch of the long pink scar on his chest. Nothing scared Remi—not spiders, not snakes, not jumping horses, not anything. But the idea that she'd almost lost Julien before she'd found him again—that terrified her. She said a silent prayer of thanks he'd survived his battle with cancer, which made this morning and every other morning she planned to wake up with him possible.

"Morning already?" she asked, pulling the covers over her breasts and sitting up.

"Unfortunately," he said. In nothing but his pale blue boxer shorts, he walked over to the bed and leaned in for a kiss. "Good morning."

"Morning breath," she said.

"Don't care," he said and kissed her hard and deep before pulling back and smiling at her. "I woke up without my stupid virginity hanging over my head. You think a little morning breath is going to bother me?"

"Your virginity was hanging over your head?" Remi asked. "And I thought hymens were weird."

Julien laughed and pulled her into his arms. Remi sighed, deeply contented despite the lingering worry in the back of her mind. She couldn't bear the thought of leaving Julien, and yet she could only stay in Paris so long before everyone back home got dangerously suspicious.

"Thank you for last night," he said, kissing her neck and her shoulders.

"I should thank you. That was amazing," she said. "It might have been your first time, but it was my best time."

"Best time? Are we talking sex or races?"

She laughed again. "Sorry. Hard to get my head out of the business."

"You really run things at Arden, don't you?" Julien stretched out next to her in bed. He slid his hand under the sheets and rubbed her hips and thighs.

"I do. At least I thought I did before all this mess. Mom and Dad have been running the show behind my back. I'm more than a little pissed off about that."

"I don't blame you," he said. "I'm pretty pissed too. I don't know how bad this could get, but I know when there's gambling and race-fixing and professional sports involved, it can be..."

"A disaster," she completed for him. "Pete Rose banned from baseball. Lance Armstrong stripped of his medals and jerseys. Reggie Bush giving back the Heisman."

"You know so much more about sports than I do."

"You're not a typical guy, are you, Julien?" Remi asked.

"In the hospital, the nurses would hang out in my room with me longer if I had soap operas on. And my sisters would visit and that's what they wanted to watch. That and *Grey's Anatomy*. I put my foot down over that one. I had enough hospital drama in my own life."

Remi almost smiled, but she saw Julien wasn't joking. "That must have been lonely," she said. "Being in the hospital all the time."

"Mom and Dad worked their asses off with the farm. My sisters were in school. I don't blame them. They loved me and visited me every chance they got. But still I was alone a lot. My brain was my best company."

Remi wrapped her legs around him. "If I had known you were in the hospital by yourself, I would have visited you every day," she said and meant it. "I would have hung out with you and watched sports with you and made sure you never ever had to watch *General Hospital*. I don't care what my parents would have said about it, I would have been there for you."

"You were there for me. Sort of," he said, and Remi noticed a faint blush on his cheeks.

He got out of bed and walked to the window seat. When he came back to the bed he held a magazine in his hand.

"That's a *Horse & Hound* magazine, Julien," she said. "You are doing porn the wrong way. Let me get you a *Playboy* subscription, please. Or introduce you to the internet."

Julien grinned and flipped through the worn and wrinkled pages. "Mom brought me her old magazines to read in the hospital. Remember this issue?"

Remi glanced at the cover. It did look familiar to her. "Yeah, I did dressage for years. I won a medal when I was twenty-two."

"And you and your team got a photo spread in *Horse & Hound*," Julien said. "Look at that."

He flipped to a page near the center of a magazine. "Who is that smoking hot chick in the riding clothes?" he asked, pointing at a smiling blonde girl in buckskin jodhpurs, a white shirt with a gold pin through her stock tie, a chocolate-colored coat, buff leather riding gloves and black riding boots. The young woman had her hair plaited in an elegant French braid and wore no make-up but tasteful pale pink lipgloss.

"That would be me with the helmet hair."

"You look so hot in this picture that for two years every sexual fantasy I had involved a girl in a dressage uniform."

"Seriously?" Remi laughed.

"Dead serious."

"I'm not showing any skin in the pic," she said, remembering the days of sweltering under that coat. "Can't see anything but my face."

"It left everything to my very good imagination. Remi...those boots..."

"You like the leather boots, huh?" she asked, giggling like she was back in college again and had nothing on her mind but boys and horses.

"I had dreams about those boots." He practically growled the words.

"So when I showed up in your living room yesterday...?"

"I was pretty sad you weren't wearing the boots."

"I still own those boots," she whispered into his ear then bit his earlobe for good measure. Julien groaned softly. "I have so many pairs of boots."

"There are horses in France," he said, sliding on top of her. "In case you want to go riding."

"I did a little riding last night," she said.

Julien laughed and buried his head against her neck. "More than a little."

"You want to try this morning?" She relaxed underneath him.

"We can do it again?" he asked.

"All you want," she said, kissing him. "And maybe later...I'll wear the boots for you."

Julien was already so eager he didn't even

take off his boxer shorts before pulling his erection through the slit and settling between her open thighs. Using her hands, Remi opened herself up for him. Julien penetrated her easily, as she was still wet from last night. She sighed with pleasure as she lifted her hips to take every inch of him.

His thrusts were slow this morning, tentative and unsure. She guessed he wanted to prolong the coupling and avoid coming too soon. He was young, new at sex, and no doubt worried about embarrassing himself with his inexperience. She adored him for it.

"Your cock feels incredible inside me." Remi ran her hands through his mussed morning hair. "In case you were wondering."

"I was," he said, his voice slightly strained.

"I love your body too." Remi ran her hands up and down his back, so lean and smooth-skinned. "Everything about you turns me on."

"Everything?" he asked between kisses.

"Everything," she repeated as he rose up and put his hands on either side of her shoulders. She opened her legs wider, cupping the back of her knees with her hands.

"You're trying to make me come, aren't you?" Julien closed his eyes tight.

"Oh, no. You're not allowed to come. Not yet."

"I almost died once, Remi. Are you trying to kill me again?"

"Only in the fun way," she said.

"The French do call the orgasm 'the little death.'"

"No dying for you," she said as he kept thrusting slowly into her. "Not until I tell you to."

"I want you to come too. What do I do?"

Remi gave him a mischievous grin. "Keep doing that. And watch the show."

He sat on his knees and resumed his hard steady thrusts. Remi slipped a hand between her legs and found her clitoris.

"Oh my God," he breathed.

"Just focus on what you're feeling," she said as she closed her eyes. "I'll focus on what I'm feeling."

"What are you feeling?"

"You inside me," she said, her eyes still closed. "The ridge on the head of your cock is really pronounced. I can feel it rubbing against my g-spot."

"Seriously?" He sounded equal parts pleased and fascinated.

"Seriously. And it's a really good feeling. When I get turned on I get really hot."

"You are hot."

She laughed again. "The other kind of hot. And my boobs feel huge. Do they look huge? When I have sex they feel massive."

Julien cupped both her breasts in his hands. "They're the perfect size for my hands."

"Then don't let go. I love feeling your hands on my breasts."

"I'll never take them off," Julien pledged.

"Good."

"Remi?" He stopped thrusting for a moment and the pause in the pleasure wrenched her back to reality.

"Something wrong?" she asked.

"No. Maybe. I'm falling in love with you. Is that bad?"

Remi raised her arms and Julien fell into them. "No," she said. "It's crazy. It's stupid. It's irrational and probably dangerous. But it's not bad. And I think I'm falling in love with you too. It scares the hell out of me, but it's not going to go away anytime soon, so we might as well enjoy it."

"Like this?" he said, with a thrust that Remi felt in the pit of her stomach.

"Exactly like that."

He kneaded her breasts as he rode her with long thrusts. As Remi rubbed her pulsing clitoris, Julien pinched her nipples and squeezed her breasts. Ecstasy washed over and through her as Julien pounded into her. Little cries echoed from the back of his throat, barely restrained moans.

She raised her hand to his face and caressed his lips. He opened his eyes and looked down into hers.

"Come," she said. "Inside me."

His head lifted slightly, his hands gripped her hard, and he came with a quiet gasp in the back of his throat.

Remi was so close to coming...so close. Julien pulled out of her but soon he replaced his penis with his fingers. He ground three fingers into her wet opening, thrusting hard into her just the way she liked it. Julien licked and sucked her hard and swollen nipples as she arched into his mouth.

Had she ever felt anything this good before? Anything this torrid and hot and wrong and right all at the same time? There was no part of her body that didn't burn with desire right now. She'd never felt this sexual, this desired, this needed...and she never wanted it to end.

Her orgasm crashed through her, every nerve firing in her back and belly almost to the point it hurt.

Spent at last, she rolled onto her stomach. Julien threw a leg over her lower back as he kissed her shoulders.

"You know what the crazy thing is," Remi said, still panting. "Sex gets better the more times you have it."

"If it gets any better, my dick is going to break off."

"We'll glue it back on."

"Boss?" Merrick's voice came through the door and the entire room rattled with the force of his knocking.

"I'm kind of doing something here, Merrick," Remi said, rolling her eyes.

"I know you're done fucking. The dishes in the sink aren't rattling anymore."

"Fine. We're done. What do you want?"

"I don't want anything except breakfast and a raise, but we'll talk about that later. You're wanted. You left your phone out here, and you have six missed calls from the farm."

"It's Sunday," she groaned.

"Tell that to the fucking horses," Merrick said.

"I'll be right out," she said.

"Put on clothes first," Merrick ordered. "And take a shower."

"Anything else, Mr. Dearborn?"

"Brush your teeth. And tell Julien to get dressed too. We need to figure our shit out."

"We have shit to figure out?" she asked.

"What's your last name?" Merrick demanded through the door.

"Montgomery."

"What's the last name of the guy you've been banging all night?"

"Point taken," she said with a sigh. "I'll be out in half an hour. Take the credit card and go get us some...I don't know. Croissants? That's what French people each for breakfast, right?"

"Way to buy into a cultural stereotype, Boss," Merrick said.

"Actually they do eat croissants for breakfast," Julien said.

"I'm not talking to you, Julien Brite," Merrick said, sounding highly perturbed. "I bite my thumb at you. You sullied my lady's virtue. And if you're anything like me, you sullied her chest and her face too."

"But it was really good sullying," Remi yelled back. "Really *really* good sullying."

"Oh," Merrick said. "Party like a cock star then. Breakfast in thirty, as ordered."

Remi showered and brushed her teeth with a new toothbrush Salena had left for her. She wrapped her wet hair into a loose bun and pulled on yesterday's clothes. The entire time she rehearsed the speech she would have to give her father about where she'd disappeared to and why she hadn't answered her phone. She was a terrible liar, especially to her parents. She was nineteen before she lost her virginity because she couldn't bear to lie to her parents about what she'd done on her dates. She'd had to wait until college. If they caught her with Julien Brite, plotting against both families, it would be a tragedy of Shakespearean proportions.

"Croissant?" Merrick tossed a bag at her as she emerged into the living room.

"Delivery. Nice," she said, digging into the bag. Merrick sat in a large dark green armchair with Salena on his lap. He was feeding her bites of croissant. Apparently she and Julien weren't the only ones who'd engaged in some naked misbehavior last night.

"Do you believe in hole-'n'-stick medicine?" Merrick asked Salena.

"Holistic medicine?"

"No, this is a different thing."

Remi coughed loudly to get Merrick's attention.

"She must need more hole n' stick medicine," Merrick stage-whispered to Salena.

"Merrick," Remi said, snapping her fingers. "You yelled at me to get out of the most comfortable bed I've ever slept in with the sexiest most amazing guy I've ever met. Focus please. What's the situation?"

Merrick focused. "Seven missed calls now," he said. "Dad. Mom. Trainer. Mom. Dad. Trainer. Last one from your mother."

"Oh God, not my mother," she groaned and collapsed onto the sofa. Julien emerged from his bedroom, fully dressed and looking adorably sheepish. Salena grinned at him, and he turned a becoming shade of scarlet.

"What's going on?" Julien asked, sitting next to her on the sofa.

"Trying to figure out what to tell my parents about where I am. I can't say I'm on vacation. That's too suspicious. I'm not the whirlwind-vacation-taking type. At least I wasn't," Remi said.

"You." Merrick pointed at her. "You aren't going to say anything to them. You're a terrible liar. Just tell me when we're going back to Kentucky, and I'll handle it. When are we going back?"

Remi shrugged. "I don't know. We can't stay here long."

"Yes, you can," Julien said, giving her an almost pleading look. "At least stay as long as you can."

"Brilliant idea," Merrick said, rolling his eyes. "I'll just run out and get us two French citizenships and a bag of money so we don't have to go back to our jobs, and we'll move right in and eat croissants and fuck all the time. Wait. That's actually an amazing idea."

"Sounds good to me," Salena said, winking at him.

"We can't stay," Remi said, smiling apologetically at Julien. It hurt to say the words but it was better to say them now, get them out, and deal with the fact of them. "I have a job. So does Merrick. And while I might be furious at my parents for whatever they're into, I can't abandon the farm. I love the horses too much."

"Gross, Boss," Merrick said.

"I don't love them like that," she said, wadding up her empty croissant bag and throwing it at him.

"You really love it there?" Julien asked.

"I do," she sighed. "I did. I liked being in charge. I liked being responsible for the well-being of the horses and the jockeys. I take really good care of them." She was speaking in the past tense and it scared her. Something told her that her days as Arden Farm's manager were numbered.

"She does," Merrick said. "Arden Farms has the lowest horse and jockey injury record of any Thoroughbred horse farm in the U.S."

"All this work I do." She stood up. "Every safety measure we've implemented, all the progress we've made...if my family gets caught by the racing commission fixing races or taking kickbacks from the track? It's all gone."

"I won't let them fuck over your work, Boss," Merrick said.

Remi smiled at him, something she rarely did. "When I was a kid, I went to Keeneland Race Course with my dad for the horse auctions. And he told me that in the 1950s, Keeneland paid for every preschooler in Lexington, Kentucky to get the polio vaccine. He told me that and I said then and there, that's what Arden Farms would be like. We would give back to Kentucky like that. And now..."

It broke her heart to even think of it, to think of all her hard work being tarnished by a scandal she had nothing to do with. She couldn't bear to face it, but couldn't hide from it forever.

"Tell my father we're in New York," she said. "Tell him we'll be back by next weekend."

"Next weekend?" Julien sounded devastated.

"I have to work," she said. "I have responsibilities. I have to take care of the farm before my family makes everything FUBAR."

"FUBAR?" Salena repeated.

"Fucked Up Beyond All Recognition," Merrick translated.

"Lovely," Salena said. "So where—"

The buzzing of Remi's phone silenced the entire room.

Remi took a deep breath. Merrick held out his hand. She winced and handed him the phone.

"Merrick here," he answered. Remi grabbed Julien's hand for comfort. She couldn't bear to look so she put a hand over her eyes.

"Remi? She's still out," Merrick said to whoever had called—her father most likely. "I know. She misplaced her phone. We just found it. Women. Am I right?"

Remi heaved a sigh of relief. Having such a bizarre assistant paid off sometimes.

"Where's Remi? She's out in the stables with this guy...I don't know his name. She got a hot tip on a couple horses."

Good, Remi thought. Dad loved it when she aggressively went after a good horse.

"What horses?" Merrick repeated. "I don't know. Brown ones?"

Remi tried to grab the phone from Merrick. He slapped her hand away.

"Any luck with the horses?" Merrick repeated. "Yeah, she's found herself a nice young colt. She rode him last night."

Julien clapped a hand over Remi's mouth to stop her from yelling at Merrick.

"How big is the colt?" Merrick said. "That's kind of a personal question. Big enough to enjoy the ride, not so big she can't walk today, I guess."

Remi glanced at Julien through a slit between her fingers. He'd fallen onto his side on the sofa and lay curled in the fetal position with a pillow smashed on his face. He was either laughing or crying. She couldn't quite tell which.

"Yeah, I'll have her try to call you once she's back in," Merrick continued. "We're getting shitty reception out here in the country so don't freak out if she doesn't call you back right away. We'll be back this weekend."

Merrick ended the call and tossed Remi the phone. "You're good," he said. "I covered your ass."

"You told my father I rode a fine young colt last night," she nearly screamed.

"What? You did," he said.

"He had a point," Julien said, waggling his eyebrows. He lay back on the couch, his ankles crossed on the armrest. All she wanted to do was drag him back to bed with her. But instead she had to think, to plan.

"Come on," she said to Julien as she reached out her hand to him. He took it and she started to pull him to his feet. "I only have a few days left with you before I have to go back. Show me Paris."

"No," Julien said.

"No? You're not going to show me Paris?" Did he really think they could spend the next few days fucking? Well, if he wanted to try, she was game.

"I will show you Paris, yes. But you aren't going back."

"Julien, I told you. I have a job. A very important one and—"

"*We* are going back," Julien said. "All four of us. Right, Salena?"

Salena smiled at Julien. "I go where you go," she said to him, a display of loyalty that made Remi love Salena just a little bit. What next? Was she going to love Merrick, too?

"And I come where you come," Merrick said to Salena and bopped her on the tip of her nose. Nope. No love for Merrick.

"It's settled then," Julien said.

"You're coming back with me?" Remi asked, her heart fluttering with the new and dangerous love she felt for Julien.

"Yes. I just got you back. I'm not going to let you go that easily this time," Julien said, taking both her hands in his.

"Julien, I don't want to leave either, but we can't be seen together. And I don't want to drag you into this mess. I can take care of it on my own. Merrick and I can, and then we'll come back here."

"I don't care if you can take care of it on your own," he said. "You're not on your own. It's my family's mess too. I don't know what the plan is, but I don't care. I'm going. We're in this together."

She sighed and then smiled. "Okay, we're in this together," she agreed. "Whatever this is. We need a plan."

"I've got the plan," Merrick said. "First I get hard evidence against your parents. Then we put the thumbscrews on them."

"How do you propose to get hard evidence?" Remi asked him.

"The usual," Merrick said. "I'll sneak into the offices and snoop. Hopefully I won't find naked pics of your mom. Again."

"Nice plan, but someone's always at our house," Remi reminded him. "And my family doesn't like you or trust you."

"My parents work from the house too," Julien said. "One of them is always at home. But I can try to dig around their home offices at night."

"Do you have any idea what you're looking for?" Merrick sounded skeptical.

"Well...no," Julien admitted.

"You know anything about gambling?" Merrick asked. "Anything about business, finance, or record keeping?"

"No."

"Are you a computer hacker and/or know

your parents' passwords to their bank accounts so you can see if you they perhaps have received payments from mysterious sources?"

Julien sighed. "Okay, you got me there."

"Then I have to do it," Merrick said. "I just have to get into your house. Is it alarmed?"

"Not when we're home."

"Cool. We'll need to get everyone in your house out of your house and we have to make sure they're in such a tizzy—"

"A tizzy?" Remi repeated.

"A hardcore stone cold motherfucking tizzy," Merrick said. "They need to be gone for several hours with no chance of them returning and walking in on me *à la* the Christmas party four years ago. I computer hack naked. It's just a thing. Don't ask."

"Then what's the plan?" Remi asked. "You have one, yes?"

"Yeah, and it's a fucking good one," Merrick said. "It's also insane and horrible and you're probably not going to go for it."

"Let us decide that," Remi said, although she truly dreaded whatever was about to come out of Merrick's mouth. If even he thought the plan was insane and horrible, she could only imagine her reaction to it.

"I'm not telling," Merrick said.

"Why not?" Remi narrowed her eyes at him. Of all times to be abstruse.

"Because you'll kill me," Merrick said, wincing. "I'll be worm food."

"Stop being a drama queen and tell us the damn plan," Julien said. Remi heard a note of command in his voice and liked it. He might be young but he wasn't weak.

Merrick raised his hands in surrender. "Fine. Stop pressuring me. I feel violated," he said. "So...the plan."

"Yes...?" Remi waved her hand to encourage further words.

"First of all," Merrick said, "do either of you know a really wicked priest?"

P aris with Julien was one perfect moment
after another.

Perfect Moment #1: Julien kissed her
under the *Arc de Triomphe,* which led to a
crowd of tourists applauding them.

Perfect Moment #2: Julien took her to the
Musee de l'Orangerie where they stood in silence holding hands as they stared into the
deep blue of Monet's water lillies. They didn't
say a word in the room. Words would have
been an insult to the lilies. Remi realized that
day she enjoyed being silent with Julien as
much as she enjoyed their conversations.
She'd never been able to say that about anyone
else before.

Perfect Moment #3: All four of them—
Remi and Julien, Merrick and Salena—spent

hours and Euros galore in Shakespeare & Company. They bought more books than they could possibly fit in their suitcases. Salena bought French novels. Julien bought history books. She bought a little bit of everything. And Merrick bought erotica. All of it. The entire section. When she lamented her books wouldn't fit into her suitcase, Julien told her to leave them at his place since she would need reading material when she came back to visit him again. That simple statement "When you come back" gave wings to her heart. They had a future together and it was so certain he was already encouraging her to leave things at his apartment.

Perfect Moment #4: Remi and Julien's last night together before she left Paris. While Julien was inside her he whispered things into her ear they never taught her in Sophomore high school French class.

J'ai envie de toi.

I want you.

Fais-moi l'amour.

Make love to me.

Je veux passer la reste de ma vie avec toi S'il te plâit?

I want to spend the rest of my life with you. Please?

To that Remi had only one answer.

"*Oui.*"

On Friday morning, Remi kissed Julien goodbye *un, deux, trois* times, and she and Merrick boarded their return flight to Lexington. She was leaving the City of Light and Julien for the Horse Capital of the World and her parents. She did not consider this a fair trade. Julien and Salena would wait a few days before following them back to Kentucky to avoid unnecessary suspicion.

Remi and Merrick barely spoke on the flight back, but he held her hand for part of the trip—a much-needed show of support and comfort.

"This is crazy," she whispered to him as their plane began the descent.

"I know," he said, and gave her that broad wicked grin that sent women either running to him or away from him at top speed. "And that's why it's going to work."

"I can't believe I got—"

"Don't stress," Merrick said, squeezing her fingers. "Just tell yourself it's not real. That helps. Now deep breaths. Focus. Eyes on the prize. We got this."

"The pep talk is not helping," she said.

"Would you rather have a hand job?"

Remi glared at him.

"Don't say I never tried to help you," he said, shoving his sunglasses down on his face.

Remi did her best to play it cool on Wednesday. Luckily her father was busy enough he didn't interrogate her about the unplanned horse-hunting trip she'd taken, seemingly on a whim. The irony of it all was that he trusted her implicitly, and she no longer trusted her father at all.

She tried to concentrate on her work that day—bills, invoices, ordering supplies, scheduling races, meeting trainers—but Julien had taken over her mind. She thought of his face, so angular and striking. She thought of his skin —so young and smooth and warm. She thought of his body and how it belonged on top of her, inside her, underneath her, and every other sexy position she could think of. She missed the light citrus smell of his sheets on her skin and his arms that had held her as she'd fallen asleep during the all-too-brief nights she'd spent in his bed.

On her way to her small house that sat on the edge of her parents' thousand-acre property, Remi's phone buzzed with a text message.

Here, the message read. Remi grinned at her phone.

Where? she wrote Julien back, desperate to see him again.

My family picked us up at the airport, he wrote. *Trapped with them. That's why I'm texting instead of calling.*

Remi stared at her phone as she unlocked her door and walked into her house. She'd lived in the house for three years now and never before had it felt empty or lonely to her. And it didn't feel empty or lonely now. But it needed something, someone else here. That someone else unfortunately was trapped at his parents' house.

I need to see you, came the next message from Julien. Five little words that made Remi's heart dance, her stomach trip, and her feet flutter.

Tell me when and where and I'll be there, she wrote back.

Mom won't let me out of her sight for a couple days. We're visiting my grandparents in Ohio. I'm being smothered.

Your fault you're so damn cute.

I love you, came Julien's reply.

That too, she replied and then added an *I love you* of her own. She wasn't used to writing those words, saying those words, feeling those words. But the more she wrote them, spoke them, felt them, the better they fit onto her fingers, her tongue, her heart.

She went to bed alone and cursed the cold sheets. She had loved sleeping with Julien. Every night after sex, he'd rubbed her back while they'd talked. Their very last night together had been their best night. They'd dared to discuss the future, a future they could share. Remi had asked Julien what he wanted to do with his life.

"I never had a dream job before I had leukemia," he'd answered as Remi curled up on his chest. She'd gotten so used to his scar by now she rested her head over it without a second thought. "So maybe one good thing came out of being sick. Now I know what I want to do with my life."

"Which is?"

"Help teenagers with life-threatening illnesses. I don't want to be a doctor. That's not my thing. I want to help them the way Salena helped me—by getting me out of the house. I don't know what to do with that dream yet, but at least I have one now. You? Do you always want to work at Arden?"

"Not anymore," she'd confessed. "The

place seems tainted now by what my parents did. I still want to work with horses, but I want to find a way to be around horses and do something with them other than running them into the ground. The best part of my job is the charity work we do at Arden, the people we help. I just want to find a way to do that as a full-time job."

"You dreams good dreams," Julien said, kissing her on the top of the head.

"You're my best dream." They'd made love again after that and fallen asleep tangled in each other. Five nights ago was the last time they'd been together. Five nights and an eternity.

She wouldn't survive another five nights and she told Merrick exactly that when he shuffled into work an hour late the next day with a big smile on his face.

"Did you spend the night at Salena's?" she demanded.

"Yup."

"You're fired."

"For getting laid?"

"Yes."

"My, aren't we sexually frustrated this morning," Merrick said, handing over her coffee.

"Five days," she said. "I'm not going to make it."

"You'll make it. If I can last five days you can last five days."

"Have you ever gone five whole days without sex?"

"Sure. Of course. Oh, you mean five *consecutive* days?"

"It's ridiculous. This isn't medieval England or Renaissance Italy. Families shouldn't be feuding."

"Tell that to Steve Harvey." Merrick asked, sitting on her desk in front of her. "It must be awful for you. Julien's forbidden fruit. Taboo. Off the menu. Verboten. The scandal? The lies? The sneaking around? Terrible."

"Awful," Remi said.

"Horrible."

"Shameful."

"It's hot, isn't it?" Merrick asked.

"So fucking hot." Remi dropped her head to her desk and groaned. Merrick, knowing what was good for him, didn't laugh at her. Not too much anyway.

Remi knew she'd tear Julien's clothes off the second she saw him again but when that would be she didn't know. Salena was still working out her end of the plan. Remi didn't want to rush things, but if she didn't see Julien again soon, she couldn't be held responsible for her actions. When she texted Merrick at midnight on Thursday, she knew that was a symptom she'd reached the end of her rope.

You awake? she wrote him.

No. I'm dead.

I'm thinking about the plan, she wrote him.

Stop thinking. Just go fuck him and let me sleep, Merrick wrote. And then for some reason added emojis of a gray alien, a skull, a bee, the flag of Japan, and seventeen eggplants.

But it wasn't a terrible idea, sneaking over to Julien's for an hour or so. Well, no. It was a terrible idea and she knew it.

She wrote Merrick back.

What if I get caught at his house?

Merrick replied with a ghost and a Santa Claus.

WTF?

Be quiet as a ghost, he explained. *Get in and out like Santa.*

I was supposed to get that message from two emojis?

Duh, he wrote back. *Go get it.*

And he punctuated his text with a rather

phallic-looking banana emoji, and that was logic that neither she nor her vagina could argue with.

She threw on her clothes again and got into her car.

Capital Hills, Julien's family's horse farm, constituted twelve-hundred acres near Frankfort, the state capital. This late at night with no traffic to contend with, Remi made it to the outside of the farm gates in thirty minutes. She parked her car on a side road and carefully climbed over the white wooden fence.

"I can't believe I'm doing this..." she whispered to herself as she crossed the dark manicured lawn. Julien had said his family only alarmed the house when no one was at home. She hoped he was right about that. "How horny am I?" she said under her breath.

Horny enough to risk a B&E conviction obviously.

"Julien, Julien," she breathed, "where the hell are you, Julien?" The windows of the three story colonial mansion were mostly darkened, but light glowed from two second-floor windows.

Did you get a fancy corner bedroom? she typed on her phone.

What? Julien replied. *Yes. Why?*

I'm looking at your window, she wrote back.

She counted only two seconds before Julien's face appeared in the window. He opened his window and stuck his head out.

"You're crazy," he whispered. In the clear night air, the words carried right down to her. Her heart, already pounding from sneaking to his house, now leapt at the sight of him.

"Crazy for you. Will your mom let you come out and play?" She smiled up at him.

"It's sixty degrees out. You come in and play."

"Where?" she asked. She'd never been to the Brite family home before. He held up his finger in the universal sign of "wait right there."

Remi glanced around while she waited, hoping the Brites didn't have any rabid killer attack dogs wandering near the house tonight.

She heard a whistle and peeked around the corner of the house. Julien stood on the back covered porch and waved her in. She ran to him, and he caught her in his arms. In a frenzy of silent kisses, Julien pulled Remi into the house and shut the door behind them. He kissed her mouth, her neck, her earlobes and throat while she ran her hands all over his bare chest. He must have been getting ready for bed because the top button of his jeans were already unbuttoned. Good. Less work for her.

"I missed you so much," Julien murmured as he nuzzled her hair.

"I really shouldn't have come, but I couldn't wait anymore."

"It was killing me too," Julien said, his hands sliding under the back of her shirt. He unhooked her bra and pulled her even tighter to him.

In the dark she could barely make out what room they were in but it seemed to be a large office or a small library. Didn't matter what it was. They were alone in it and that's all she cared about.

Julien dragged her skirt up to her stomach as he kissed her wildly. Blood pounded through her. Her thighs felt tight and her stomach knotted itself up as Julien slid his hand into her underwear.

He found her clitoris with his fingertip and rubbed the swollen knot until she had to bury her mouth against his shoulder to keep from moaning audibly. She dug her nails into his back, holding onto him with everything she had. She shuddered hard in his arms when he pushed two fingers up and into her. Wet as she was, he slid right into her.

"I won't make it to my room." Julien rasped the words into her ear.

"Then just do it here."

Julien was fantastically good at taking orders—one good quality among many. He wrenched her panties down her legs and turned her back to him. During their nights in his Paris apartment, she'd done everything she could to help him make up for all the time lost while he was sick. She let him try any sexual position he wanted. Quickly they discovered together that Julien loved entering her from behind. She loved it too but at this point she wanted him so much she'd strap them both to the roof of a moving car if that was the only way she could get it.

"What if your parents walk in on us again?" she teased. She heard Julien behind her unzipping his jeans.

"I locked the office door."

"What if they break in?"

"I'll tell them to wait their fucking turn then."

He pulled her skirt up again and pushed his fingers into her. Remi arched her back and braced herself against the wall as he opened her up for him. Behind her Julien guided himself to her entrance. She pushed back and felt the head bumping her g-spot. Remi sighed with the sheer relief of having Julien inside her again. She arched her back even more to take all of him inside her. He bottomed out and started thrusting. This was exactly what she needed.

"I can't get enough of you," Julien said as he pulled out all the way to the tip and crashed back into her. She forced herself to stay silent as he emptied her and filled her with each thrust. He slid his hands under her shirt and cupped her breasts. All Remi could do was hold herself still against the wall as Julien slammed into her again and again, the sounds of her wetness and his labored breathing accompanying his every move.

Her climax built quickly and she came hard, her inner muscles fluttering and clenching tightly around Julien's still thrusting length.

She went limp in his arms, and he pulled out of her. He turned her to face him and she wrapped her arms around his neck. He kissed her again, delving into her mouth with his tongue. He was backing her up as he kissed her. She didn't know and she didn't care where he was taking her as long as he was taking her.

Something hit the back of her legs, and Julien lowered her down onto a leather sofa. He yanked her shirt up to expose her breasts and sucked hard on her nipples. He hadn't come yet and she wanted him to, needed him to. For six beautiful nights she'd fallen asleep with his semen in her and on her, a privilege she'd never granted any man before. They didn't use condoms simply because he'd been a virgin and was sterile. She'd known the moment she saw him that she wanted to give him everything she had and keep nothing from him.

Julien kissed his way down her stomach.

"Julien—"

"I have to taste you," he said. He held her by the back of her thighs and Remi obediently opened her legs for him. If he had to, he had to. Who was she to argue?

He licked the seam of her vagina from base to apex and down again. The leather couch creaked under them as he devoured her with deep and hungry kisses. He pushed his tongue all the way into her before focusing his attention solely on her clitoris. He licked it gently, sucked it greedily, and rubbed it until

Remi couldn't stop herself from coming again, even harder this time. Her hips rose a foot off the sofa and as she came in dead silence, every part of her vibrating with pleasure.

She collapsed in a daze. Julien pushed between her legs again and entered her fast and hard. He went wild on top of her, fucking her as if he'd die if he stopped. Spent and drained she could do nothing but lie beneath him and take his every rough and hungry thrust. She watched his face, studying the beauty of it. His eyes were closed to concentrate better on his pleasure and his dark eyelashes fluttered on his cheeks. His face was flushed with desire, and his skin had pinked like a rose. Quiet breaths escaped through his slightly parted lips and a swath of his unruly dark red hair fell over his forehead. He'd told her that he'd grown his hair as soon as he could in a sort of victory lap against the leukemia that had robbed him of it. She'd promised she'd never make him cut his hair as long as they lived if he didn't want to.

Reaching up, Remi swiped the lock of hair off his forehead and grazed his cheek gently with the back of her hand. His eyes flew open and he gazed down at her. He bore down on her and with his eyes locked on hers, came inside her, filling her up all the way to her heart.

She smiled at him when the last of their frenzy had died down.

"I love you," he panted. "I keep thinking I'll get to the bottom of what I feel for you. And then I do and the bottom's just a lid and I open the lid and there's more love inside it. Was that stupid? I can't tell if it's stupid or poetic."

"It's perfect. And I feel the same way," she said, taking him in her arms. She felt his heart beating wildly against her own chest.

"I guess that's a good thing," he said. "Considering."

He laughed and the laughter shook her body and his.

"Exactly," she said. "Merrick is crazy. This plan of his is crazy."

"But it's going to work, right?" Julien asked.

"We'll make it work."

Julien pulled out of her and winced.

"Are you hurt?" she asked.

"No...just wet. And the couch is leather. And Mom sits here all the time."

"Oh no."

"Don't move," he said. Don't move? Of

course she wouldn't move. She clamped her thighs tight and waited for Julien. He came back with a box of tissues, and helped her with the cleanup.

"Six tissues," he said. "Wow."

"Impressive." They high-fived. "You've been saving that up for awhile, haven't you?"

"I was very close to taking matters into my own hands. Thank God you showed up and saved me from myself."

"I knew there was a reason I did something this stupid. It was all for you," she said as Julien balled up the tissues. She got up and found her abandoned underwear and pulled them on while Julien opened a side door. She heard a toilet flushing. Good. Smart way to dispose of the evidence.

"I should go," she whispered as he came back to her with his jeans now zipped and his hair somewhat tamed.

"No way. Not yet," he said.

"We can't get caught. And we're already pushing our luck here."

"My parents sleep like the dead. Stay for a little while, please."

"Will you show me your room?" she asked, grinning at him through the dark.

"Upstairs. Now," he said and he grabbed

her by the wrist. Luckily most of the house was carpeted so they made almost no sound as they raced upstairs to Julien's room. When they reached his room she had to cover her mouth to stop herself from laughing uproariously. Julien's bedroom was a time machine. It was as if the year 2006 had been isolated and preserved in this one bedroom. A *Batman Begins* poster hung on the wall. A *V for Vendetta* poster hung next to it. A large CD player and two foot high speakers sat on a table. She hadn't owned a stereo system that large in years. An Eminem CD and a Dave Matthews Band concert DVD lay side by side on top of the stereo.

"Wow," she breathed. "Am I in the past?"

Julien locked his bedroom door behind them. "Sort of."

"I like it. But then again, I had a big Christian Bale crush back then."

"Such a girl," he said rolling his eyes. "It's about Batman's toys. And that he doesn't use guns. Or kill people."

"And Christian Bale."

"Girl."

"Boy," she said. "Did your mom keep your room like this is a shrine?"

Julien laughed and pulled her to his bed—

a full-size bed, thankfully. She'd worried it would be a twin.

"No," he said. "I was just too sick to care what posters were on the walls. The house has ten other guest rooms so mom's in no hurry to redecorate. And now I've moved out so who cares what's on the walls?"

"Have you thought about living with me?" she asked. "I mean, once we go through with this plan."

"At your house on your parents' land?" He sounded dubious.

"Actually, I have a better idea. Tell you when this is all over."

"I'd live on the streets with you, Remi."

"Don't worry. I'm foreseeing much nicer accommodations for us. So you'll move in?"

"I love you," Julien reminded her. "And we're in this together."

"I love you too. And I promise, this is going to work. And no one will keep us apart ever again. "

She kissed him so he would know she meant it. And she did mean it. This love had charged into her life, kicking up clods of dirt with fierce and flying feet. She'd never expected it, never saw it coming, never knew what hit her. She'd been run over by a team of wild horses, and she couldn't be happier about it.

"You know," Julien said into her lips, "I always wanted to have sex in my own bed at home while my parents were sleeping."

"You rebel."

"Want to?" he asked, pushing her onto her back again.

"Oh no, anything but that," she said, throwing her leg over his back.

Julien slid on top of her and the bedspring creaked loudly.

And at that moment, someone knocked on his door.

Remi froze, her heart racing. She looked around wildly trying to find somewhere to hide.

Julien only rolled his eyes. "Great timing," he sighed and stood up.

"What are you doing?" she rasped.

He smiled at her. "Show time."

He opened the door and Salena stepped inside his room. She had a cup of ice in her hand for some reason.

"Am I interrupting?" she asked, one elegant eyebrow arched at the both of them.

"We're done," Remi said.

"We weren't done," Julien said, "But I guess we are now."

"I got off the phone with my friend at the hospital," Salena said. "Now's the time."

Julien exhaled heavily and nodded. "Okay. Let's do this," he said.

"Open up. Time to lower your temperature." Salena popped an ice cube in his mouth and Julien sucked on it. "And you should go. This place will be crawling with people soon."

"We'll walk you out." Julien placed his hand on her lower back. "This probably shouldn't happen in my bedroom anyway, or they'll wonder why Salena was in my room at one in the morning."

They returned to Julien's mother's office and Julien opened the door that led to the back porch. She wrapped one arm around his back and kissed him.

"No, no," Salena said. "We want to lower his blood pressure, not raise it."

"Oops." Remi pulled back. With one private smile at Julien she whispered, "See you on the other side."

He kissed her forehead, and she left him and Salena alone in the office. The last thing she saw was Salena shoving a needle into

Julien's arm and Julien collapsing onto the floor. No going back now.

As she drove away from Capital Hills, two ambulances and a police car passed her. She knew exactly where they were going.

Julien and Salena were doing their part. Merrick would do his part tomorrow. Only one thing left to do now.

Her turn.

At dawn, Remi got out of bed like usual, got dressed to go riding, and headed to the stables. She rode often at work. Arden Farms was so large that workers drove golf carts between the stables. She much preferred to saddle one of the working horses and ride wherever she had to go—usually one of their three Tennessee Walkers. This morning, however, she picked Benvolio. There wasn't a horse on the property that could jump like Benvolio could. Perfect.

"Don't be mad at me," she whispered to Benvolio as she tightened the girth. "I'm going to do something very stupid, but I won't let anyone blame you."

She fed Benvolio an apple and stroked his long nose.

"You won't get turned into glue for this, I promise," she said, brushing a tangle out of his mane. "I'm crazy in love with someone and you're going to love him too when you meet him. So just trust me, okay?"

Benvolio didn't answer with anything but a nuzzle against her shoulder. She took that as a sign she had him on her side.

She stepped into the stirrup and swung her leg over his back. With a twitch of the reins he started down the path toward the practice track. She warmed Benvolio up with a few small jumps. Good. They could do this. As she neared the track she saw her father leaning against the fence like he had for as long as she could remember. Coffee cup in hand, newsboy cap covering his bald spot, and an intense look of concentration on his face as two of their strongest four-year-olds pounded down the practice track.

They passed the finish line and she saw her father hit a button his stop watch. Finally he looked away from the track and noticed her. She waved at her father. He waved at her. And just as he was starting to look away again, Remi gave Benvolio the signal to break into a canter. With a shift of her weight, he obediently jumped. Well-trained as he was, the horse obeyed. Even though she knew she'd have one hell of a bruised ass from this little stunt, Remi let go of the reins and fell from the saddle.

She hit the grass with a thud that rattled her teeth. Any other time she'd been knocked off a horse, she'd get right back up again. But not today. Today she was on a mission.

Instead of getting up, Remi closed her eyes.

Only seconds later she sensed herself being surrounded by people, nervous and scared. She heard her father's voice shouting for a doctor. She heard one of the trainers saying they should call 911 immediately. People called her name, patted her face, tried to pry open her eyelids. She lay there as best as she could, pretending to be unconscious.

Ten minutes later, she was in the back of a speeding ambulance. Her father had yelled he'd follow right behind in his car. As she was being loaded, she pretended to come to just long enough to ask her father to bring her mother too. He promised he would.

Now it was on.

As soon as she was alone in the ambulance with the EMT's, she miraculously recovered and started talking. The EMT's said she'd be checked at the hospital for a concussion and monitored for a few hours. Of course she would. She knew exactly what would happen once she got to the hospital. In her twenty-six years she'd fallen off a horse and bumped her head half-a-dozen times and had gone through this routine every time. She hated that she had to scare everyone like this, but she knew Merrick was right—this was the only way to guarantee both of her parents would be away from the farm long enough for him to do his digging. The guilty feeling gnawed at her, but considering her parents had involved the farm in possibly illegal activities, she decided giving their parents a brief scare was a fair trade for the hell they'd put her through.

Luckily, at the ER she was considered a low priority patient as she was awake, alert, and seemingly unharmed. She was shunted into a side room and semi-forgotten. Every fifteen minutes a nurse would peek in the door and make sure she was still conscious. The nurse asked if she wanted her parents back in the room. She politely declined the offer. Instead she turned on the television and found nothing on but soap operas.

So this is what Julien went through for

years—sitting alone in a hospital room staring at a television and waiting for his life to start.

Finally, Merrick texted her.

Got it, was all the text said plus a rocket ship emoji.

Get here, she wrote back and just because she loved him a little bit today, she added a smiley face.

And a banana.

Half an hour later, Merrick walked through her hospital room door. He had a file folder in his hand, two ledger books, and a sheaf of printed pages.

"Is that it?" she asked as he sat on her bed and tossed the papers in her lap.

"All of it." He wore an ear-to-ear grin. The only thing that made Merrick happier than getting into trouble was getting someone else into trouble. "Read."

She read through everything he'd brought her. On the one hand she was thrilled they had hard evidence. On the other hand, she was more furious than ever.

"I'm going to kill them," she said once she'd finished reading.

"We're in a hospital. Good place for a heart attack," Merrick said.

"They might try to kill me," she said.

"I won't let them, Boss. I'd kill for you, die for you, I'd even take a bare bodkin for you."

"You'd take a dagger for me?"

"I thought a bare bodkin was a penis."

"It's a knife."

"I've seriously been misreading the subtext of *Hamlet* then."

"Come on. We have two sets of parents to freak out."

She grabbed the pile of papers and together they found her parents waiting in the lobby. Her father was on his phone, no doubt checking in with the farm. Her mother was flipping through a magazine without making eye contact with any of the pages.

"Good news," she said to them. "I'll live. No concussion."

"Oh thank God," her mother said, and reached out to hug her.

"You gave us a little scare there," her father said, stoic as always.

"I'm about to scare you two a little more," she said, refusing to return the hug. Merrick's find had implicated not just Julien's mother and father in this mess, but both her parents as well. "Merrick, what room is he in?"

"He's in 5515," he said.

"Who? What are you talking about, Young

Lady?" her father asked, narrowing his eyes at her. "And is that my ledger book?"

Remi took a step back and crooked her fingers at her parents. "I have someone you two need to meet," she said. "I think you'll like him."

The elevator ride to the fifth floor was a bit awkward, but Remi refused to answer any of her parents questions. *You'll see...*was all she said. Out on the fifth floor they walked past the nurse's station. A young nurse demanded to know whose room they were visiting.

Remi sighed. She was afraid this would happen. That's okay. She had this.

"Julien Brite, room 5515."

"His parents have requested family only can visit."

Remi grabbed a sheet of paper off the nurse's station desk and scrawled a few choice words onto the paper and handed it to the nurse.

"Oh," the nurse said. "Go right in."

"Thank you," Remi said.

"Remi Anne Montgomery, you tell us right now what is happening," her mother demanded.

"Julien Brite?" her father repeated.

"Young lady, didn't we tell you that you were never to see him again?"

"You did. I ignored you." Remi pushed open the door to room 5515. Julien was sitting up in bed surrounded by his family. She nearly teared up at the sight of him in the hospital room. Hopefully this would be his last trip to a hospital for the rest of his life. Instead of crying, she kissed Julien.

"Excuse me, miss," came a woman's voice from behind her. Remi ignored it. She looked Julien in the eyes.

"Did we get it?" he whispered the question. He could have shouted it if he wanted to. Everyone in the room had recognized each other at once. Her parents were fighting with his parents. A nurse shouted over them all to shut them up. And in her peripheral vision she saw Merrick standing to the side and taking pictures of the melee and grinning.

"We got everything," she said and gave him one more long, lush kiss.

"Excuse me?" Remi felt a tapping on her back. She stood up, turned around and faced Mrs. Deidre Brite. "Just what do you think you're doing?"

"I was just slipping the tongue to your son," Remi said with a smile.

"You were what?" she gasped.

"It's okay, Mom," Julien said. "Remi and I are sleeping together so she's allowed to kiss me."

"Julien!" his father yelled.

"I'm going to need everyone to shut up and sit down right this second," Remi said. "Or stand. I don't care. But you all do need to shut the hell up because Julien and I have a few very big announcements."

Julien hopped out of the hospital bed and stood at her side. Just then Salena in her white doctor's coat and blue scrubs entered the room and stood by Merrick. Good. They didn't want her to miss the show.

"Announcements?" her father said. "You drag us to a hospital to tell us you're dating Julien Brite? Remi, what the hell is going on here?"

"First of all, you should know Julien and I are fine. Neither one of us is sick or injured. We faked it to get you away from the farms so Merrick could do a little digging. He struck gold, in case you were wondering."

"Julien, you scared your mother and I to death—" Mr. Brite started but Julien raised his hand.

"Yeah, well, you all scared me a little too

by engaging in illegal activities. I think faking a faint is barely a misdemeanor considering you all are committing felonies," Julien said.

"What are you talking about?" Mr. Brite demanded, his face red and angry.

"We'll get to that in a second," Remi said. "The second thing you need to know is that Julien and I are together. And that's the least of your problems."

"Problems?" Mrs. Brite repeated, looking nervously at her husband.

"Big problems," Julien said. "Remi, you know this stuff better than I do. Can you explain it?"

"Happily," she said. "You see, Tyson Balt owns Verona Downs. And Hijinks and Shenanigans are the favorites for the Verona Downs Stakes race. Everybody bets on the favorites. If they lose and one of the long-shots wins, Tyson Balt and Verona Downs will be swimming in money. Mr. Balt paid our parents ten million dollars each to whip the press into a frenzy over the biggest horse racing rivalry in decades and then throw the race. Neither Shenanigans nor Hijinks will win and Balt will be richer than God."

Remi held up a series of emails Merrick had printed out. "I've got emails from Balt to everyone in this room about the race fix. Don't even bother to deny it."

"Remi, honey," her mom began.

Remi held up her hand. "I don't want to hear any excuses," she said. "Do you know how much trouble you all could be in if the racing commission found out about this? Do you?"

All four parents remained silent.

"Do you have any idea how humiliating this would be if the scandal broke? It would be all over the racing news for weeks. Arden and Capital would become laughingstocks and pariahs. Pariahs," she repeated, knowing how much her family and Julien's cared about public opinion.

"And all for what?" she continued. "Money."

"That money is your money too," her father said. "We did this for you and the farm. Do you have any idea how expensive it is to run a Thoroughbred farm?"

"Of course I do," she said, pointing at herself. "I'm the damn farm manager, Dad. I know we're doing fine. We're not billionaires, but nobody's starving around here. And did you really think I wouldn't notice what an ass you all were being in the news? That stupid feud should have never started to begin with. Julien and I got a little carried away, but it was nobody's business but ours. Did you think I would just stand by and let you all drag our good names through the mud? Did you think I wouldn't notice you all bought the new farm and paid cash? Do you all think I wouldn't notice the Brites dropping ten million at the auctions? How stupid do you all think I am?"

She waited. No one wanted to touch that question. Wise decision.

"Here's the thing," Remi said, and took Julien's hand in hers. "I had my suspicions, and I needed someone in the Brite family to help me confirm them. Julien did. And in addition to helping us get all this lovely evidence, he and I, well, how would you put it?"

"We're in love," Julien said. "Madly and completely in love. For starters."

"What do you want with us?" Mr. Brite, Julien's stern father, asked.

"That is a fantastic question," Remi said. "And luckily we have a fantastic answer. Capital Hills has a nice crop of yearlings. Arden just bought a second farm. You're going to give me and Julien the yearlings and the farm. We'll sell the yearlings and you all can call it a donation. Oh, and we want Shenanigans and

Hijinks too. You all don't deserve those horses."

"You want what?" Mr. Brite asked, utterly aghast.

"A plague on both your horses!" Merrick shouted.

Remi turned around and glared at him.

"Sorry," he said. "I always wanted to say that."

"We want your ill-gotten gains," Julien said. "And we're going to use them for good. Remi and I are going to turn the farm into an equine therapy non-profit to help sick, disabled, and poor teenagers. And you all are funding it. Congrats. Criminals to philanthropists in one afternoon."

"We are, are we?" her father asked, sounding both angry and skeptical. "I'm not entirely sure I'm on board with this plan."

"Tough shit," Remi said. "You lost your vote in this matter when you put our entire farm and our family's reputation at risk. You all should be ashamed of yourselves. And even if you're not, you're going to make amends for it anyway."

"She's so sexy when she gets tough like this," Merrick said.

"Totally agree," Julien said, and he and Merrick fist-bumped.

"The Brites and the Montgomerys can't simply start a non-profit together," Mrs. Brite said. "We're incorporated businesses. And the rivalry in the press—"

"Is over," Remi said. "Done. Finished. Kaput. It's history. Now and forever. And you all will be holding a press conference in one week to announce to the world that the feud is over. The Brites and the Montgomerys have forgiven each other. The press will eat it up. Then you'll announce that the creation of Shenanigans—a day camp that will be funded by Arden Farms and Capital Hills for needy, sick, and disabled teenagers. And you won't be taking another cent from Tyson Balt ever again. You won't be betting money on horse racing ever again. And you won't be throwing another race. Ever. Again."

Remi paused and let the words sink in.

"And if we don't?" Mr. Brite asked after a minute's pause.

"Your son and I will be giving the racing commission a call."

"You'd turn on us? Your own family?" her father asked.

"Me? I'm the one turning on the family?"

Remi was aghast. "You got greedy and put our good name and reputation at stake. Julien and I could have just called the commission. Instead we're giving you all a way to exit this idiocy with grace and dignity."

"I don't even know who you are anymore. This isn't the Remi Montgomery I know and love," her mother said in her most scolding tone.

"No, it isn't," Remi said. "Because I'm not Remi Montgomery."

"What?" her mother gasped.

"She's Remi Brite," Julien said with a wide victorious smile. "We got married in Paris. Merrick took pictures."

"They're right here," Merrick said and held up his iPhone. "Doesn't Remi look pretty in her dress? I picked it out. Oh, and here's the marriage document/license thingie." He held the certificate up for the room to see. "*Voila!* That's French for '*voila*.'"

"It's a good thing we did get married," Remi said, turning to kiss him quick on the mouth. "The nurse said family only was allowed in your room. I wrote her a little note that said I'm your wife and these are your in-laws."

"Hi, in-laws," Julien waved at the room.

"You got married?" Mrs. Brite breathed, staring bug-eyed at her son.

"I know it's a little sudden," Julien admitted, wincing. "But it was the best way to guarantee... What did you call it, Merrick?"

"A merger," Merrick said. "And these two crazy kids have been merging like crazy. In your house last night even."

"I can't help it," Remi said without apology. "I missed my husband."

"My daughter and Julien Brite got married," her mother repeated. "Married? Married to Julien Brite?"

"Say 'married' a few more times," Merrick said. "It's starting to sound like 'Merrick.'"

"It was definitely a wedding. There was a French minister, and we were in a church and it was all quite romantic," Remi said, her voice strong and true. True because it was true—the church, the flowers, the ceremony. "Sorry you missed it."

Her mother looked at Remi, then Julien, then back at Remi, and sat back down in her chair. But she didn't faint so that was good.

"Are you telling us the truth?" her father demanded. He stared her straight in the eyes. Everyone knew she always choked when she had to lie to anyone.

Remi calmly faced her father.

"Church. Minister. Wedding ceremony. Me. Julien. Vows. Document signed, sealed, and..." She grabbed the document from Merrick's hand. "Delivered."

She gave the marriage certificate to her father.

"You're not lying," her mother said, looking wild-eyed at the document.

"Mom, you've been telling me for two years to find a nice guy and settle down. I found the nice guy. We're settling down. And yes, it is sudden and shocking, but it is also the smartest thing I've ever done."

"Can't wait for the honeymoon," Julien said.

"Will you marry me?" Merrick said to Salena.

"Absolutely not," Salena said.

"Why not?"

"You're bizarre, arrogant, and insufferable."

Merrick didn't seem at all surprised or disappointed. "We can keep fucking though, right?"

"That goes without saying."

Remi's mother had her hand on her forehead. Her father looked like he might throw up. Julien's father and mother were arguing with each other. No one was having a heart attack.

She'd call it a win.

"Want to get out of here, Mr. Brite?" she asked Julien.

"I've made a miraculous recovery overnight, Mrs. Brite," Julien said.

"And you did say something about a honeymoon," Remi said.

"Any suggestions?" Julien asked as he shoved his feet into his shoes and grabbed his jacket.

By the next morning, all four of them were on their way back to Paris.

R emi and Julien's parents didn't speak to them for nearly three months. It wasn't so much that Remi and Julien had extorted million of dollars from them. The families admitted they'd been greedy and in the wrong. But Remi and Julien had waited until the day after the press conference to tell their parents the truth—their wedding in Paris hadn't been legally binding.

Remi was never quite sure what Merrick had said to the French minister or how much he'd bribed him to perform the wedding and sign off on a semi-official-looking document. She didn't know and she didn't want to know. The ruse of the wedding had been for her sake anyway. Merrick knew Remi would never be able to lie to her parents with a straight face

and say she'd gotten married if she hadn't actually gotten married. She knew they weren't
legally married but it was enough that she
could look her mother in the eyes and say she
and Julien had a wedding. It was a dirty trick
to convince their parents that they had no
choice but to give up the rivalry now that the
only Montgomery daughter had married the
only Brite son. If the two families had merged,
the two businesses were merged whether they
liked it or not. Remi and Julien considered this
little hoax of theirs nothing more than payback for the high-priced and dangerous fraud
their parents had been perpetuating.

With their parents still not speaking to
them, Remi and Julien spent Christmas Day
alone together. But the privacy suited them
just fine as Julien asked her to marry him on
Christmas Eve. They celebrated her "yes, yes,
absolutely yes" by making love under the tree.

Twice.

By New Year's, their families jointly for-
gave them at a dinner party Remi hosted.
Remi wanted to believe this forgiveness was
born of their parents seeing the error of their
ways, repenting, and turning over a new leaf.
In truth, she knew it was the reams of good
press that Capital Hills and Arden Farms had

gotten all over the world that had changed their minds. The "moving, touching, awe-inspiring" decision to bury the hatchet and create a children's charity that would let sick, disabled, and needy children spend time riding and caring for horses would cement the Brites' and the Montgomerys' legacy of giving and service to Kentucky and the horse racing world. Every racing family in the tri-state area had stepped up and pledged money to the cause. The Raileys had already written them a check for five million that their parents accepted in an embarrassingly staged photo op at Verona Downs.

Remi didn't take it too personally that her parents and Julien's parents were taking all the credit for the idea of the charity and acting as if this merger had been their plan all along. All Remi cared about was Julien, her horses, Merrick and Salena, and their plans for the future.

And getting her fiancé into bed.

Right now.

In November, they'd moved into their new place—the farm her parents had, against their will, given them for the non-profit. By January it already felt like home. Julien had started school again at the University of Kentucky and was working toward a degree in psychology so he could better help the kids who would be served by their charity. At age twenty-six, she was officially engaged to a college freshman and she couldn't be happier about it. Remi had set up an office for him in the rambling Victorian house that had come with the acreage. He looked so cute sitting at his desk, hunched over his textbook and laptop that all she could do was stroll in and stand there waiting for him to notice her.

The wait lasted about one second.

"Oh damn," Julien said, sitting back in his chair. He stared at her wide-eyed.

"I told you I still had the outfit." She'd put on her old dressage clothes for him—tan jodhpurs, leather gloves, velvet coat, white shirt with tie, and of course, the riding boots.

"I can't breathe," Julien said.

"Should I call Salena?" Remi batted her eyelashes. "Or should I just take the outfit off?"

"Option B, please." Julien got out of his chair and came to her. He cupped the back of her neck and kissed her with bruising force.

She pulled away and grabbed him by the hand. They'd had office sex shortly after moving in. Some things were better left to a big comfortable bed.

Once in their bedroom, Remi shut and locked the door behind her. Merrick had been wandering around earlier, and she didn't want him wandering into their bedroom by accident. Knowing him, it wouldn't be an accident. She pushed Julien down onto his back and straddled his hips.

He put up no fight whatsoever.

"I love the braid." Julien tugged on the end of her French braid.

"Easiest hairstyle to fit under a helmet," she said as she unbuttoned his shirt. She ran her gloved hands all over his bare chest.

"Plus I can do this," he said, gently tugging on her braid to pull her head back. He rose up and kissed the exposed flesh of her neck.

"Even better." She purred the words as she kissed him again, long and deep and with all the love and passion she felt for him. And she did love him, and knew she would love him forever. The stars would burn out long before her love for him did.

Once more she pushed him onto his back. She unzipped his jeans and wrapped her gloved hand around him.

"That is weird," he said, gasping slightly.

"Never had leather on your cock before?"

He shook his head.

"Never. I kind of like it though. Maybe." He narrowed his eyes. "No, wait. I definitely like it. No, I love it."

She rubbed him gently, feeling him getting harder and harder with every long stroke. Julien propped up on his elbows and watched her touch him. Well...if he wanted a good show, she could give him a good show.

Remi sat back and lowered her head, taking him into her mouth.

Julien collapsed onto his back with a groan.

"Oh my God..." he breathed. "Blow job with you in riding clothes... Teenaged-Julien is somewhere in the past with a massive hardon and a smile on his face and he has no idea why."

Remi didn't answer. Her mouth was a bit too busy to speak at the moment. She ravished him with her tongue, licking him from base to tip and back down again. She tasted the first drops of his semen. Good. She wanted him to come in her mouth. He'd been working so hard today. He deserved it.

She gripped the base and worked her mouth up and down his length. At first she went slowly to tease him. Once his breathing hastened, she moved faster to coax him to the edge. She loved hearing him pant for her, loved seeing his eyes closed and his lips parted and his fingers digging into the sheets of the bed they shared and made love in nearly every night. She hoped that somewhere out there their parents were quietly fuming that she and Julien had won. Life was undeniably good right now and was only getting better.

In a few months, life would get even better than it was right now, and she couldn't wait to tell him why.

Julien's breathing quickened as she sucked him deep into her mouth. He said her name once and then came with a rush, his shoulders coming off the bed from the reflex of pleasure.

She swallowed every drop of him and wiped off her lips with the back of her gloved hand.

"You are the sexiest woman alive," Julien breathed. "It's ridiculous. If you got any sexier, I don't think I'd make it."

"No?" she asked, as she got off the bed and pulled off her boots. "What if I did *this?*"

She slipped out of her jodhpurs.

"The world becomes a better place when

you take your pants off," Julien said, watching her every move.

"What if I did this?" She stepped back into her boots and zipped them up.

"You without pants on and wearing boots is..." Julien paused.

"What?"

"Well, it could only get better if—"

Remi slithered out of her panties and tossed them onto Julien's chest.

"That," he said.

She straddled his hips again and rubbed herself gently against him.

"I'm not going to make it," he said. "You're so sexy it's killing me... I'm going...going..."

On the "gone" he grabbed her and flipped her onto her back. In a tangle of arms and legs and laughing, Remi ended up with her head hanging off the bed and Julien between her thighs. Good place for him to be, the perfect place even.

With quick rough fingers, Julien unbuttoned her coat and the white shirt underneath. He kissed her breasts as he gently teased her clitoris. When he'd grown hard again, he pushed deep into her.

And because she knew he would be disappointed if she didn't, Remi crossed her legs at the ankles and rested the heels of her riding boots on his lower back.

"Even better," he whispered.

"Even better what?" she asked.

"Your boots on my back during sex is even better than I dreamed it would be."

"It really is," she agreed. "This was a good idea."

"The best idea. I think this is the new best day of my life."

"It's about to get better," Remi said.

"How?"

"Because we've got a baby on the way."

Julien froze mid-thrust.

"A baby?" He stared at her, his eyes huge with shock. "But...they said I couldn't have kids. And I'm still in school. And we aren't actually married. And we haven't talked about... but still, that's-"

"Not me, silly," she said, and smiled up at him. "I'm not the one pregnant."

"Not you? Then who?" Julien looked so wildly relieved she almost laughed at him.

Remi patted the side of his face.

"Shenanigans."

———

ABOUT THE AUTHOR

 Tiffany Reisz is the *USA Today* bestselling author of the Romance Writers of America RITA®-winning Original Sinners series.

Her erotic fantasy *The Red*—the first entry in the Godwicks series, self-published under the banner 8th Circle Press—was named an NPR Best Book of the Year and a Goodreads Best Romance of the Month.

Tiffany lives in Kentucky with her husband, author Andrew Shaffer, and their two cats. The cats are not writers.

Subscribe to the Tiffany Reisz email newsletter:

www.tiffanyreisz.com/mailing-list

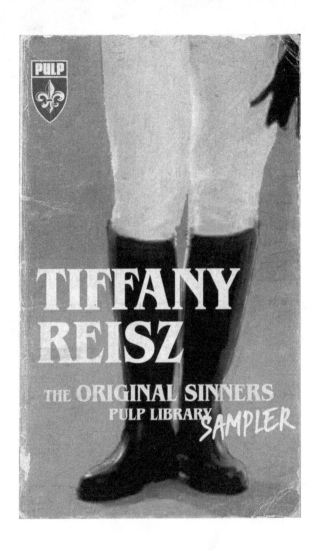

FREE ebook sampler at www.tiffanyreisz.com
or wherever ebooks are sold.